Gunny's Pups

Rebel Wayfarers MC
#10.25

I0619378

MariaLisa deMora

Edited by Hot Tree Editing

First Published 2017

ISBN 13: 978-1-9467380-4-2

DEDICATION

There is no pain so great as the memory of joy in present grief. ~ *Aeschylus*

For my gorgeous and goofy Ratty, Beetle.
It's true, when we're owned by a dog,
we become better people.

CONTENTS

Chapter One 1

Chapter Two 29

Chapter Three 46

Chapter Four 75

Chapter Five 103

ACKNOWLEDGMENTS

If there's one thing I've learned from Gunny, it's to listen when he's demanding to be heard. From the beginning of his journey with us when he attempted to take over Jase's story, earning his own book through sheer persistence, to his on-screen parts in books like *Secret Santa* and *Bones*. And now to this story, *Gunny's Pups*.

I think one of my favorite things about Lane Robinson as a character—other than how noisy he can be when he wants something—is the growth our Gunny has shown.

Here's hoping he has a few more good stories in him. I kinda like where he takes us.

Woofully yours,
~ML

Gunny's Pups

Chapter One

Gunny

"Sharon." Gunny bellowed his old lady's name up the stairs. *Where the fuck has she gone?* "Gotta get my ass in gear and out the goddamned door. Need my fuckin' kiss. Get your ass down here."

"Coming." The single word was soft and sweet, and the sound of her voice had his cock at half-mast in a moment, thinking of how she'd called out this morning as he rode her hard. *Gunny, I'm coming.* Muffled into the pillow, he'd still heard her, had known it wouldn't be long once one of her shoulders dipped to the mattress. Then he'd felt the heat from her touch against his slapping sack as she'd worked her clit, the combination of his slamming thrusts and her clever fingers pushing her over the edge.

"Fuck." Tipping his head back and closing his eyes, he took a deep breath, trying to will his erection away. "Don't have time for this." The moment those words hit the air, his eyes popped open and then he was taking the stairs two at a time on his way back up to where Sharon was. "Fuckin' liar. Always have time to play with my woman."

Forty-five minutes later, as he made his way slowly back down the stairs, he reached behind him so he could cup Sharon's ass. Her head rested on his shoulder blade, legs wrapped as far around his waist as they'd go, arms twined around his neck. "Love you, big guy." Her languorous murmur was soft but sweet, and when he squeezed her cheeks, she giggled. He heard that and felt it, the shaking of her body echoing through his chest.

"Love you, too, baby." Backing up to the couch, he released his hold, letting her slide down to stand on the cushions. "I seriously gotta get goin' now. PBJ's gonna be waiting on my ass as it is."

"Did he give you any idea what he wanted?" She tugged at his arm, pulling him around so he faced her. From her position on the couch, she was still shorter than him, so he swooped down the few inches to capture her mouth with his. Silenced by his kiss, her question went unanswered as he slanted his head and touched his lips to hers softly.

"Gotta go. Call me if you need me or if Cade needs anything." Quick clicking noises came from the kitchen, and he glanced in that direction to see one of their dogs trotting through the door. Squinting slightly, he thought the dog's head looked odd, then as the beagle came closer, he realized the trash can lid was stuck around its neck. *Shit.* "Baby, thinkin' you might wanna check the kitchen. Tank's been in the trash again."

"Not my Tank. He's a good dog." Loyal to a fault, Sharon defended the clearly guilty culprit, then peered around Gunny and got a look at the canine. "Is that green on his face? Green, smushy...avocado?" She sighed, giving up on the pretense that Tank wasn't the world's worse sneak. "Bad dog." While Rocky, the rat terrier, could pick goodies out of the tall garbage pail without making a mess or leaving any evidence, Tank was true to his name, always bulldozing over obstacles like trash cans. Gunny knew Sharon would find a mess when she went into the kitchen and decided it wasn't the time to answer her earlier question, given what he knew about PBJ's ask.

Gunny stared down at Sharon, taking in again the beauty that smiled up at him. Hair flowed down her back in sleek sheets, her bright eyes curving with the grin that stretched her full lips wide. "Love you, babe." Pressing his palm against her belly, he gently stroked the swell that protected their second daughter. "Fuck, but I love you."

Now her eyes were bright for a different reason, and she sniffed when she scolded him, "Don't be sweet to me. You know how I am these days." She'd become more sentimental the closer they got to the date, which was only a couple of months away. "You make me cry, you need to make me come again to make up for it." Shaking her head, she sniffed again. "And while we'd both enjoy that, you're already late."

Leaning in, he kissed the tip of her nose, then stepped back. "Wouldn't wanna have to make you come again." His fake grousing made her smile, her broad grin matching his. "See you in a bit, baby. Call me, yeah?"

"Yes, sir." Snapping a salute, she stepped off the cushions and to the floor. "Who's a bad boy," was directed to a thoroughly garbage-rumpled Tank who'd thrown himself in front of the couch and had a nearly-matching expression on his face, tongue lolling out in his doggy grin. She was still reprimanding the dog as Gunny closed the door leading into the garage, cutting off her voice in midscold.

***

Lifting a fist, Gunny turned the doorknob with one hand while he pounded on the door with the other, walking in and announcing himself in the same movement. "PBJ, where ya at, brother?" A wordless call barely audible over the cacophony of barking from deep in the building gave him a direction, and he allowed the door to swing shut, darkness enveloping him.

The address hadn't been one Gunny knew, and from the outside, the house didn't look remarkable. A sprawling single-story ranch, it had several outbuildings and one large pole barn out back.

Inside, it was a nightmare. Dark doorways leading into shadowed rooms, dim hallways that went five strides and turned deeper into the house. A hundred enemies could be hiding within ten feet of him, and he wouldn't see them. Not until they were close enough to touch, close enough to strike. *Close enough to kill*.

Back pressed against the wall nearest the door, Gunny stood and fought the same demons that had chased him for so many years. Fought and won, as he did more often these days.

Sharon, he thought, letting his eyes close so he could better remember the scent and feel of his woman. Body in front of him, little spoon curved into the crook of his legs, the slow, smooth way they shifted and moved together, cock buried deep inside her, pulling out to the tip before smoothly rocking forwards again.

Her hands on his face, drawing his mouth up to hers as she rode him fast and hard, her weight no burden at all. Him thrusting up into her even as she was dropping her ass against his thighs until the sound of their flesh slapping together echoed in the room.

Hair matted with sweat, eyes fixed on their tiny daughter, her exhausted face radiant with love and a determined satisfaction at giving him something they'd both wanted so badly. *Sharon*. He let the knowledge that she loved him seep into his bones until he could move again.

Licking his lips, surprised at how dry they were, Gunny opened his eyes to see Deke and PBJ standing across the room. From the wary expressions on their faces, he knew his struggle had been apparent, which would be one of the reasons they were over there and no closer. "Hey," he grunted, rolling his shoulders to ease the tension from his muscles. "Got a beer?"

"Pope wear a funny hat?" PBJ grinned before he turned and walked up one of the hallways leading off the room. A living room, Gunny realized. Large and made for a big family, it had to be half the length of the house. To his right was a wall of windows, papered over now, blue painters tape securing the newsprint in the opening, protecting glass and woodwork from whatever would be slapped on the walls.

"You good, brother?" Deke's quiet question wasn't a surprise. He knew how deep the scars dug into Gunny's soul, and seemed to have a knack for popping up at the moments he was most needed. "Bad?"

"Not too. Just a...momentary lapse." Gunny wiped at his sweaty face with the crook of one elbow. "I'm good. You know what PBJ needs us for?" Pushing off the wall, he went to follow PBJ, stopping when Deke's hand gripped his bicep. "Brother, I'm good."

"Sharon okay?" Deke shook his head, stopping Gunny's response. "Of course she's okay, or you'd be there and not here, but…are you okay with…fuck, man. You cool with having two little ones?"

At that stupid, senseless question, Gunny finally found it inside himself to laugh, chuckling aloud at the expression Deke wore. "Yeah, I'm good. More than good. Can't wait for Cade's little sister to be sleepin' down the hall. Kitten brings us full circle, man. *It's all good*." Hoping Deke understood the emphasis, he knew his friend got it when his grip tightened on a squeeze and then fell away.

Before Sharon, the lasting effects from Gunny's time serving in the military overseas had nearly overwhelmed him on a daily basis. Episodes would drive him to the forest for weeks at a time, in a useless effort to escape.

Post-traumatic stress disorder was so much more than an acronym to him, and Deke knew more than most the stress Gunny had lived with for years. Since finding Sharon, Gunny's entire world had changed in so many ways. Not the least was him moving her into his house, a sanctuary that only a few had seen before she'd instigated the first barbecue thrown in their backyard. Heavily pregnant with Cadence, their first daughter, Sharon invited everyone she knew mattered to him, and they had shown up with platters of food and baby gifts in hand.

So many memories with her, he thought, following Deke to the back of the house, frowning at the growing level of sound as they got closer to the source of the barking.

"Fuck." The exclamation was pulled from him as he looked around the large room off the kitchen. Row upon row of crates and cages, nearly all of them filled with dogs. The smell was overwhelming, so many of the animals had been left contained too long, forced to urinate or defecate in their living space, some of them multiple times. "Fucking hell, PBJ, what kind of bullshit is this?" Angry on behalf of the helpless dogs, Gunny swung to look at his friend's face, some of that emotion falling away as he saw a matching rage exposed on PBJ's face.

"Bitch ran off." Gunny shook his head, not understanding the statement. "Gal I was fucking," PBJ elaborated. "This was her deal, she told me she was dog sitting for people." He swept his arms out to the side, indicating the cages and animals. "Fuckin' dog sitting, and I didn't question her. She's run off, got herself sideways with a goddamned dealer, so she bailed and hit the road. Bitch called me this morning to ask me to come over and," he scoffed, the sound rough and angry, deep in his chest, "let the dogs out."

Deke spoke up, "We'd just gotten here, Gunny. Had no idea what we'd be walking into. Backyard is worse, man. She hasn't picked up shit in weeks, maybe months. Some of the cages aren't big enough for the dogs, man. We gotta do something."

"Pound?" Gunny made the obvious recommendation. "They can try to match pups to owners from her paperwork, right?"

"Ain't found paperwork on anything except a couple of the dogs. Ain't sayin' there aren't folders in some drawer, but we call the pound, and then we gotta explain how we got here." PBJ shook his head, disgust clear on his face. "I was fuckin' her, man. I feel responsible." He would. PBJ was a respected breeder and the source of both of Gunny's pups. "I wanna make this right."

Gunny studied the room for a minute. "Gotta be forty dogs, man. Where you gonna find homes for alla them?" He walked to a cabinet and picked up a lightweight slip leash, threading the fabric of the lead through the ring, making a loose noose. "Gonna start walkin' 'em."

He pointed a thick finger at PBJ. "You think. I'll do the grunt work. Deke." He glanced across the room to where Deke was making the same motions. "Sounds like we're keeping this local. Wanna call the clubhouse, get some prospects out here to clean up the shit?"

With a grin, Deke nodded, pulling his phone from a pocket. "Good job for Hurley, man."

Gunny shook his head. "You needa stop ridin' that boy. He's a keeper."

"Don't I know it," Deke agreed, laughing. "He's stepped up and done everything we've asked. No demand too big, no chore too shitty. He makes it through this, I'll know it more."

***

"Jesus, man. I'm beat." Gunny leaned his elbows on the countertop that separated the kitchen from the rest of the huge room that spanned the back side of the house. "We've done a fuck of a lot today." He cataloged the few crates still in the room, only six out of forty-five. Thirty-nine dogs had gone home with Rebel Wayfarers members and friends today, and while he couldn't be certain they were all long-term homes, they were at least clean and loving ones.

"No doubt." Deke walked towards the counter and bent over. Gunny heard a liquid swishing sound, and then Deke came up with a dripping can of beer in each hand. "We got a few left to deal with, though."

"Yeah." Gunny let his gaze sweep the crates. Six dogs, each offering a unique challenge that meant not just any owner would do for them. "Vet's picking up three of 'em, right?"

Deke nodded, popped the top on his beer. He lifted it to his mouth and took several long swallows. "Shepherd's got dysplasia, bad. If he can't be made comfortable, vet'll put him down. Maltese has an eye infection. Treatin' that, and then he'll try to place him." The veterinarian was a friend of PBJ's, and willing to look the other way at how these dogs had been acquired, having been briefed on the full situation. "Dalmatian might be blind. Vet'll decide what to do with her."

Gunny looked down, opening his own beer. "Hate that shit, man." He shook his head. "Coulda been worse, I guess." The sheer number of dogs that had been in the house would have overwhelmed the county facilities, and they weren't anywhere near a no-kill shelter. Most of the animals would have been considered unadoptable and given the barest amount of time to sit in a row and watch people pass them by. Many people adopted puppies, for obvious training reasons. With a puppy, you didn't have any bad habits to fix. With an adult dog, you might get a winner or a nightmare. He shook his head again. "Outta forty-five dogs, only three in question. Not the worst odds. Leaves us three to place, though."

He lifted the can, letting the nearly warm liquid wash away the dryness in his throat. Having to look at the crates had been running the edge of his nerves all day, bringing up harsh memories of an endless ride across a foreign desert, cooped up in the back of a truck, covered with a tarp. As helpless in his own way as these dogs had been, carried to a place where he had no friends. All control stripped away, subject to the temperament of the man driving the truck. Thank God he'd been friendly and had helped Gunny get back to Camp Chesty in short order.

"Sucks to be left behind." The bitch who'd run off had honestly been dog sitting, because every animal looked and behaved like a pet, but they'd only found a few bits of info on a bare handful of dogs. That meant that any of the dogs that had family out there were probably forever lost to the ones who had entrusted their pups to the bitch. Racked up a debt she couldn't fix and then bailed. "Abandoned." Like he'd been, behind enemy lines, his entire patrol killed in a firefight they had no hope of winning, ambushed from behind as they worked their way to the extraction point.

Gunny rolled his shoulders, feeling the hard tenseness of his muscles in response to the memories. *Doesn't do any good to get worked up like this*, he reminded himself. His phone buzzed, clattering on the counter in front of him, laid there after his last text exchange with Sharon. **Just checking in.** He smiled. **All good, big guy**.

Be home soon, he responded, and then grinned wider at the string of smiling face emojis that were her response.

"I'm gonna take the Great Dane," Deke said suddenly. "Mercy agreed, fuckin' finally. She was scared Graham is gonna be afraid of him, but I talked her around." Mercy was Deke's woman, and Graham, their young son. "PBJ's takin' the Swissie, said he's got a line on a rescue organization that'll be all over the beast as soon as he can get word to them." If PBJ was taking the Swiss mountain dog, that left only one final problem pup.

Gunny turned his gaze to where the enormous lump lay in the shadows of a large crate. Standing almost three feet tall at the shoulder, the Mastiff had to weigh upwards of 150 pounds. Intelligent eyes had studied Gunny earlier as he approached the crate with a leash in hand. He'd looked from the tiny leash to the massive dog with a laugh that had the dog perking up his ears. The pooch had walked like a prince on the lead before politely waiting while Gunny got the door open and then paced patiently outside until he found a section of yard that was appealing. He hadn't balked at returning to the crate, either, which was in contrast to how many of the dogs had reacted to having their moments of freedom curtailed.

His phone buzzed again, and he saw a picture of Sharon, her lips pushed far out in a pout. Unlocking the screen, he saw he'd missed a text and scrolled back up to read, *Just bring the big guy home already, big guy*.

"You talk to my woman today, motherfucker?"

He typed out, *The fuck you talkin about?*

That got him another picture in response, one of the sad-eyed mastiff staring through the wire grate of the crate.

"I didn't speak to her, nope." Deke's lie was plain, and Gunny couldn't help but laugh. "Might have texted her a couple of pics." On cue, another picture came in, one of him in the backyard, mastiff on the laughable leash, Gunny bent over and scratching the dog's massive head. "And might have suggested y'all need another furbaby."

"Asshole." Gunny sighed. "Lemme put him in the yard, and we can load his crate in the van. Gonna eat me outta house and home, and I got another kid on the way, man. You're cold, brother. Cold."

***

"Jesus," Gunny groaned and rolled into Sharon, curling his arm to pull her closer, listening to the rolling advance of thuds up the stairs towards their bedroom. "He can't even walk quiet."

He'd gotten home last night, and per his texted request, Sharon had their two dogs sequestered in the den, locked behind a gate. He'd kept the mastiff on the leash, letting Deke wrestle the crate in single-handedly, Sharon seated on the bottom steps of the staircase, Cade in her arms.

One of his fears had been put to rest immediately when his dogs didn't react to the strange animal except with calm interest. Even Tank, who could get wound up tighter than a yo-yo, had stood with a wagging tail and snuffling nose, waiting. Introducing the dogs through the gate had been a success, but Gunny hadn't released his two smaller dogs until later, waiting for the rest of the greetings to be done. *Isn't it interesting*, he'd thought, *that I'm already thinking of them as a trio of large and small*. As he'd walked the dog across the room to where Sharon sat, Gunny had watched as her eyes widened.

"He's huge," she'd whispered, one corner of her mouth quirking up. "It's gonna be like having a pony." The other corner of her mouth had lifted, and he'd watched her smile at the dog. "I always wanted a pony."

Shaking his head, he'd grunted in amusement. "You're fuckin' funny, woman. Reach your hand out, let him smell you." She had, and the mastiff hoovered her hand, snuffled all over it, and pulled on the end of the lead for the first time. A thread of fear had snaked through Gunny's gut at the relentless strength shown with these movements.

The dog had forced another step forwards, then another, willing to choke himself to get closer to Sharon, and Gunny had found himself along for the ride, watching as the dog lifted first one and then his other front foot to the bottom step where he immediately laid his broad head across Sharon and Cade's laps. The dog had taken a big breath that Gunny'd echoed, and something in Gunny's chest had twisted painfully as he saw lines of stress and strain flow out of the dog's muscles. Relaxed and easy, the dog had taken in another huge breath and then blown it out on a loud sigh that had made Cade laugh. At the sound, the dog's ears picked up, and he'd shuffled a half step closer to the pair he'd pinned on the stair step, gaining a couple of inches in a clear effort to get as close as he possibly could to the mother and child.

"He likes me," Sharon had whispered, trailing one hand over the dog's head, pushing and scratching at the loose skin around his ears. Cadence had squealed and thumped her tiny fists solidly on the dog's head, and the only thing that moved were tiny muscles around the mastiff's eyes, squeezed tightly shut. "You think he likes me?"

"Fuck, yeah." Gunny had matched her whisper, not wanting to break the spell, enthralled watching the scene in front of him. A tiny woman and smaller child, massive dog positioned protectively in front of them, taking comfort from their every touch. "He's home."

The first good-natured disagreement about the dog surrounded a name. Sharon wanted to pick something immediately, just pluck it from the air, but Gunny wasn't in favor of that. She'd thrown out word after word, some of them hilarious, trying to find anything that Gunny or the dog would latch onto, and came up dry.

Cadence had been in her highchair, Sharon positioned at her side to assist with the more difficult spoon-fed portions of dinner when Gunny had realized they had a problem as he called the dogs over for treats. Before leaving the house-turned-horror-kennel he'd ascertained the dog knew basic commands of come, sit, and stay, as well as down and wait, but beyond that hadn't found anything that triggered interest in the dog's attitude.

So when he'd called the dogs, he'd spoken a general, "Sit," letting them array themselves in a seated semi-circle in front of him, amused that they'd placed their asses in order, smallest to largest. "Rocky, down." A quick prone position earned the rat terrier a finger-fed snack of dry kibble, and the dog's crunching satisfaction had been loud in the kitchen as he'd eaten his reward.

Next in line had been the beagle, and when Gunny had said, "Tank, down," he'd been nonplused as two furry bellies hit the floor. "Good down," he gave verbal encouragement, then bent to offer kibble to each dog in turn. Back to a general, "Sit," he'd watched as all three dogs returned to their haunches, attention fixed on him.

Pointing with a finger, he'd indicated the mastiff, and said firmly, "Down." The dog stretched out, paws in front, weight balanced on bony elbows against the hard floor. "Good down," he'd rewarded verbally as he handed over the kibble treat. "Sit." Reaching out, he'd ruffled the dog's skin, fingers working through the folds under his chin. "Good dog."

Turning to the beagle again, Gunny had grinned to see him sitting patiently for a change. Usually, the little dog was a tornado of activity. "Tank, down," he'd ordered, and again the beagle and mastiff landed on the floor. "Fuck me," Gunny had muttered as Sharon laughed. "His goddamned fucking name is Tank."

Now it was morning, and Tank was apparently headed up the stairs. Stairs he shouldn't have been able to get to because he had spent the night in his crate. Gunny sighed, squeezing Sharon again, feeling her body starting to shake. "You laughin' at this shit, woman?"

"No," she said, the laughter in her voice giving the clear lie to her word.

Gunny's focus shifted, and he lifted on one elbow, twisting to look at the door. "It's quiet." He waited, listening. "Too quiet." The infant monitor sparked to life, sounds and noises coming from a room down the hallway. Thumping and then a loud giggle, Cade was awake and happy. "Fuck." Tank had turned the other direction and gone straight to their little girl's room. Another giggle, then the sound of furniture legs moving across the wooden floor, then the bouncing of mattress springs and bright laughter from Cade.

Gunny released Sharon and swung his legs off the bed. Out the door in two strides, he headed up the hallway. Cade's door was open, and he could hear her giggling through the opening. Reaching out, he palmed the wood and shifted, pushing the door open wider. Standing in the doorway, he looked around the room to see the mastiff lying inside the crib on the mattress, Cade draped across his back. She was pushing with her feet to rock back and forth as if the dog were a kid-sized teeter-totter. The ottoman for the rocking chair had been shoved over beside the crib, and the dog had clearly used that to give himself access to Cadence. "Jesus."

At his voice, Tank's head lifted swiftly, and the dog shifted so he could see the doorway. Gunny watched as the dog recognized him and relaxed again, laying his head down with a soft groan. Gunny felt a hand at his waist and shifted slightly to one side so Sharon could squeeze in beside him. "Awwww, he loves her already."

"Yeah, he does." Gunny sighed. "Wish we knew his background. Where he came from. I like how he is with her," Gunny shifted, pulling Sharon in front of him, "but we need to keep our guard up, baby."

Twisting in his arms, Sharon looked up at him with a confused expression on her face. "Why, honey?"

"They're a great breed, mastiffs. Protective as shit. Calm, good natured. Loyal." He paused a moment, looking for the right words. "But we don't know what's happened to him. We don't know anything about him, except he's a good dog."

"He's a good dog, and he loves Cade."

In the crib, the big dog had eased onto his side, giving Cadence a larger playground on his ribs. She was taking advantage of it, dragging herself up so she could tug and pull at the dog's ears.

Gunny grinned. "That he does." Clicking claws sounded from the hallway, and he felt the brush of fur as Tank pushed past him and into the room. Paws to the side of the crib, the beagle surveyed the scene and wagged his tail, clearly approving. Back on four paws, he turned in place twice before throwing himself to his side, tongue lolling out in another doggie laugh.

***

"Tank the Larger, that's what Sharon's calling him now." Gunny shook his head, transferring the phone to his other hand, wiping greasy fingers on the leg of his jeans. PBJ laughed, and Gunny grinned. "You should come over and check it out. He's hilarious to watch with my other pups."

"And he's still good with Cadence, yeah?" Wonder, not concern, colored PBJ's voice, and that made Gunny grin, too.

"Gentle as a lamb. Smart as fuck, though. Motherfucker opens his crate like nobody's business, and Sharon's convinced he's figured out how to open doors, too." The dog probably had. That was the only real explanation for how he'd managed to get into Cadence's room every morning through a door Gunny knew he'd closed securely. "You have any luck with finding where he came from?"

PBJ had spent the past couple of months reaching out to mastiff breeders he knew of, trying to find one who had placed a male in the Fort Wayne area. Gunny wanted to check with local vets, but Sharon had stoutly refused to look for Tank's owners, arguing he was safe and cared for, and loved, so why should they look to get rid of him?

"Not a bit of it, man. Looks like you're stuck with him." Gunny smiled at PBJ's words. *Not stuck so much as gifted.* "You coming to the clubhouse tonight?"

"Yeah." Mason, the club's national president, had called an all-member meeting to go over changes he was putting into place for one of the chapters out west. "Cleaning up now. I'll head over in a bit." He shifted, leaning one hip against the workbench. "Gotta say, I'm a fuck of a lot easier leaving Sharon here with Cade knowing that big motherfucker's in the house with my two girls."

"How long until you'll have three?" Barking on the phone followed by a quiet command of sit told him that PBJ was doing his own chores before heading into town. He lived on a ten-acre farm with a huge barn he'd converted to a kennel, transforming several of the paddocks into arenas for agility and obedience training. PBJ's facilities were in constant use by 4-H and youth clubs, as well as breed and event teams.

"Doc said he'll let her go another six days before inducing. She's not having it, and started walking laps around the house as soon as we got home this morning." She'd exhausted herself within minutes and was currently napping alongside Cade on the couch. "She's ready. I'm ready, too."

"I bet. See you at the clubhouse."

Call disconnected, Gunny pushed off from the counter and looked down to where Rocky was curled up on his garage bed, eyes opened a slit and angled up to see what his master was doing. "Let's go inside, boy." With a sigh and a stretch, Rocky trotted to the door, looking over his shoulder as if to say, *What's the holdup?* "I'm comin', gimme a fuckin' minute, Rock."

***

Gunny stood against the back wall, shoulders propped against the surface as he looked out across the sea of faces. Most were known, men he'd offer up anything if they asked because he knew he'd get the same in return. Those were his patch brothers, lined up shoulder-to-shoulder with every member of the club. Some were closer yet, like Deke, and Captain, Sharon's brother. Men he trusted no matter what was going down, he'd run uncaring into the breach knowing they wouldn't just have his back but would be striding beside him. He eyed a man standing near the front door of the clubhouse, meeting late arrivals. Mason was a man he was oathbound to protect, and someone he willingly followed.

The men Mason currently greeted with lifted chin and arm clasps weren't club; they weren't brothers. They were friendly, a club with roots down in Florida who wanted to foster better relations between the clubs. Mason had recently found family in the panhandle and, with all due respect, reached out to the dominant club in the area, letting them know he'd be in and out of the area while he built a relationship with his newly discovered sister, Justine Morgan.

A Fed in the family, Gunny thought with a snort. *Jesus wept*. Justine worked for the FBI, and until she'd recused herself from the case, had been investigating the motorcycle club founded by their father and grandfather, Shooter and Morgan. *Tangled webs*.

Gunny lifted his beer, sweeping the room again over the top of the bottle.

"How you doin', brother?" PBJ settled in next to him, raising his own beer to his lips, using the bottle to mask his words. "What the fuck do you think *he's* doing here?" The emphasis was for Pike, a Rebel chapter president from St. Louis who'd walked in the door in front of their special guests and was currently pouting near the bar because he wasn't the center of attention.

"Fuckin' diva needs his ass handed to him." Gunny had made no secret that he didn't like Pike, didn't trust the man, and wouldn't work with him unless forced.

"Why you got such a hate on for the man?" PBJ glanced over, tipping his chin to a prospect roaming with a bucket of cold beers, grabbing two from the container when offered. "Never seen you take a dislike to someone like that."

"You know Harddrive, right?" PBJ would, the old school biker had come to town last year when a revered Rebel member died, his blood brother, Bingo. For most members, it had been the first introduction to the old man, but Gunny had been buying motorcycle parts from Harddrive and his son for years. PBJ nodded. "Pike is his brother-in-law."

"Serious?" Frowning, PBJ shook his head slowly, side to side. "Mason ejected Pike from the wake for Bingo."

"Yeah, because Pike got sideways with Harddrive."

"Don't make no sense, brother. Pike's a patch. Harddrive, good man he is, ain't Rebel." PBJ held out one of the beers and Gunny reached out and took it. He spun the lid off, catching it in his hand before shoving it in his back pocket. *Old habits*, he thought, remembering the times spent picking up his brass.

"Makes all the sense when you know the history. Pike's always had a problem keeping his dick in his pants. Way I understand it, he tripped and stuck his dick into some strange pussy at Harddrive's boy's wedding, but there was a mixup, and Harddrive's old lady got told it was him who did the fucking. Caused a rift that lasted years." Gunny felt his face heating. *Asshole shouldn't be here tonight. Don't need his brand of shit.* "Years, man. Pain on pain, piled on Pike's doorstep. Wasn't until Bingo's wake that Harddrive's girl, Dixie, learned the truth of what happened. She told her momma, and by Christmas, Erin and Harddrive were back tight. Still." He shook his head, sucking hard on the bottle, swallowing a mouthful of beer. "Years. Pike's a motherfucking piece of trouble waiting to fuckin' happen."

They stood in silence for a moment, then PBJ said softly, "Jesus. Had no idea."

"Yeah, motherfucking diva piece of shit." Gunny flexed his hands, stretching his fingers wide, then clenching around the beer. "Wonder what the fucker's doing here tonight. Guests we got, it can't be a call-in from Prez."

"Yeah, I hear ya."

Mason looked up and gestured, pulling members, and officers close. Lifting his voice, he told the group, "Officers in the back now. We'll be out in a bit. Let you know what's decided." When Pike made a move to head with the rest of them, Mason called out, "Pike, local and nationals only, man." The exclusion wasn't softened by any additional information, and no honorific followed Mason's short words. Pike's nostrils flared, and Gunny thought he could hear his teeth clenching from across the room.

"Sure, boss," Pike said finally, turning away and giving Mason his back, something that made Mason's face go hard. "I'll get the lowdown on local pussy from the boys here."

Gunny, along with the dozen other Rebel officers, dropped his phone in the metal box held open at the entry to the room. Slate stood next to Hurley, ready to intervene if anyone balked. When all devices had been deposited, Hurley locked the box and handed the key to Slate. Inside, Gunny waited near the outside windows, visually ensuring Myron's tech devices were in place and humming along, blocking any listening from outside. *Hell of a thing we got here*.

"Brothers, friends." Mason stood at the head of the table, and Gunny felt the weight of his gaze when it fell on him. "We got business to deal with. Pull up a chair and get comfortable. From my perspective, we're here for the duration." The group milled around another moment or two as friends greeted each other warmly, the men from Florida more cautiously, finally settling into the chairs arrayed around the table. Gunny kept his feet, as did Slate, positioned on opposite sides of the table, bracketing where Mason sat.

One of the men from Florida made a noise and Mason gestured towards him, inviting speech. Lifting his chin, the man whose nameplate said Sparks over the word President got straight into the reason for the meeting with his opening words. "You came on my plot and shit. Didn't know better, woulda thought you were shitting on me. As it was, you left me a hella calling card with your name all over it. Then"—he made a move with his hand, fingers exploding away from his thumb—"poof, like it never happened. But you and me—" Sparks leaned forwards, angling his body towards Mason. "—we know that kind of shit never really goes away. Tell me what the gain was and I'll decide if I'm gonna leave it alone."

Mason eyed the man for a moment, a thoughtful expression on his face. "You showed respect, coming up here like this. Coulda demanded I make the trip down, and I'd a been happy to do that thing. Shows respect, though, and I gave it back—" He gestured towards the man's vest. "—because you're sittin' here wearin' your colors at my war table. Damn few folks can say they've done that." He leaned back, elbow over the back of his chair, arm swinging freely, showing his comfort level with every gesture. Other palm out, he asked, "That really what brought you here? Something we could have discussed over a secure line?" He shook his head, and Gunny watched as the visitors all tensed up, on guard in a way that was unmistakable. "No, I believe you got some significant troubles of your own, and you think to marry our causes." Sighing, Mason tipped his head to the side. "Outriders and Diamante, you got your helping of misery with the rolling patches through your plot. So much more than me coming in to clean up my own shit, regardless of the location. And Sparks,"—he shook his head—"you know that's exactly what I did. You didn't have anything to deal with that one because my boys did the cleanup right."

Gunny watched the man's expression change, moving away from disdain to something else before a grin lit his face. "Damn, Mason. I heard you were a hardass, but fuck, man." He shook his head. "From what Retro told me, I expected a little give."

"Oh, I got plenty of give in me, for friends." Mason shifted in his seat, elbows on the table now, thick forearms propped on the edge. "That what we are now, Sparks? We friends?"

Nodding slowly, Sparks turned his neck, sweeping the face of every man in the room. "Yeah. I see only friends at this table—" He paused for a moment, then tipped his head to the side as he considered Mason before finishing with, "—brother."

Mason didn't move a muscle, sat still and quiet as he kept his gaze on the man. Then with a dark chuckle, he leaned forwards, reaching out to grip Sparks' hand.

"Brother." He returned the word, and Gunny took a breath in relief.

That turned the tide, and forty minutes went by with a rapid exchange of stories and information. This was the kind of detail that Mason's Rebels needed to plan their next steps against the Diamante and Outriders, and every man had something to offer, illustrating to the Florida club that Mason knew what strengths he needed to bring to the table.

A knock had Slate on the move. He unlocked the door, stepping into the opening to block the line of sight of whoever had interrupted the meeting. A moment passed, and Gunny heard him swear. Then Slate turned to face him. "Slinky's got some trouble, brother."

Slinky's was a club-owned strip joint north of town, and Gunny was head of security for that location as well as a few others in the vicinity. If there was trouble his team couldn't handle, then he was the one on call for dealing with whatever, or whoever it was. "On it," he muttered, tipping his head to Mason and getting a chin lift in response on his way to the door. A handful of breaths later, he was through the main room and on his bike, rolling north to see what kind of problems had found a roost.

Chapter Two

Sharon

Humming softly, Sharon stood at the kitchen sink, arms buried to the wrists in hot water as she deftly washed their lunch dishes. A delicious smell filled the kitchen, and she sniffed appreciatively. With a club meeting going on, she knew it was highly likely Gunny would be late for supper, so earlier she'd put a roast in the oven. Glancing over, she saw there were about thirty minutes left on the timer. *Just enough time for a tiny nap*, she thought, flinging water droplets from her fingers into the draining sink.

"Come on, Rocky," she called quietly, knowing the terrier would hear her. As she turned towards the door, she heard the tapping of his nails on the tile floor as he got up from the bed in the corner. Tank the Smaller was sprawled at the bottom of the stairs, keeping watch on the lower half of his domain and she grinned to see him so comfortable and quiet. Since Gunny had brought Tank the Larger home, the beagle had settled down in ways she hadn't expected. "It's like you grew up overnight, Tankers." Bending, she groaned and had to flex her legs to get down and run her fingers over his head. "You could meet me halfway," she complained with a laugh, straightening and pressing a hand to her side, absently rubbing away a sharp ache that had been coming and going for the past few hours.

Stepping over him, she started up the stairs, each step seeming to take more effort. *Jesus, woman.* Halfway up the flight, she paused and bent over slightly, puffing out quick pants of air. "Kitten, honey, can you take up just a tiny bit less space in Mommy's tummy?" Pushing herself to start up the stairs again, she made it to the top step when the pang in her side returned, this time sharp enough to make her wince. Fingers pressing and rubbing on the area did nothing to ease the pain, and she felt lightheaded. Twisting in place, she put her butt on the top step, feet on another and hands to the floor behind her, leaned back, trying to stretch out what she expected was a complaining ligament.

The pain didn't ease, and she tipped her head back, going down on her elbows when it intensified instead. "Crap." She muttered, staring at the ceiling. Blinking fast, she stayed in that position, forcing away the stinging tears, finally pulling in a deeper breath as the band of iron started to ease.

"Crap. So tired now." *If I lay down here, I'll never get back on my feet.* Turning her head, she saw the larger of the two Tanks standing next to Cadence's door, looking at her with his intelligent eyes. "Hey, buddy." He blinked. "Cade sleeping?" At the girl's name, his massive head swung to the side so he could see into her bedroom, then back to Sharon. "Must be, or you'd be in that crib with her." He hadn't stopped any of the behaviors they'd seen that first day, and she loved how he wanted to be close to her baby girl.

Sharon struggled to get up, gripping the edge of the step to pull herself upright. She felt wet between her legs at the same time the pain returned with a rush, running her to ground with nowhere to hide. Sharon groaned, stuck in a bent over position, staring down at the growing red stain on her leggings. An iron force clamping across her back and swollen belly didn't give her any room to breathe, and by the time it eased, the edges of her vision wavered. "Eff," she whispered, tentatively reaching down to touch, fingertips coming back covered in blood.

She considered her options for a moment, trying to block the panic from rising in her throat. *Something's wrong.* From where she sat at the top of the stairs, it was about thirty feet to their bedroom. She couldn't remember if the house phone was in the cradle next to the bed, because she and Gunny had the habit of leaving it wherever they were when they hung up on a call. Her other option was down, and it was twenty-eight stair treads to the floor, then another twenty feet to the kitchen where she could see her cell phone lying on the countertop. As if to mock her it rang, buzzing loudly against the tile.

Another cramp threatened, and she leaned back on her elbows again, hoping it wouldn't be as bad. She was wrong, and when it eased after what seemed an eternity, her hairline was wet with sweat. She looked to the side, surprised to see the big dog right there. "Hey, Tank." He moved closer, snuffling her face, hot breath and wet tongue swiping across her cheek. "Yuck," she complained softly, not really minding. Closer yet, and he leaned in, putting his chin on her shoulder, sniffing under the fall of hair at her back. The pain returned, and she groaned, lifting an arm to circle his neck, holding tight while he pressed close.

"Tank, I need a phone." The contraction had eased, and she pushed herself away from the top of the stairs, working her way on her ass towards the bedroom. Cadence picked that moment to wake from her nap, chortling and babbling away and Sharon watched in wonder when Tank turned with only a single look over his shoulder at her as he moved towards where Cadence was in her crib.

She felt weak, struggling to move a few inches at a time and she grumbled, vowing, "Soon as Kitten is out of me, I'm going to start dancing again." Tank appeared at the edges of her vision and Sharon startled, even more surprised when he stayed beside her even when Cade's babbling turned into yelling, and then screaming, his attention focused on Sharon instead of the child. "I can't do the stairs. Can't." She was frozen in place by another contraction, arm again looped around Tank's neck to hold herself up.

It eased, finally, and she got her palms to the floor, scooting backwards, ignoring the swath of red left on the floor. Cadence's screams grew louder, and Tank shifted, glancing back and forth between Sharon and her room. "Go to our girl, Tank. Good boy." He disappeared again, and Sharon dropped her chin to her chest as another pain hit. Using the swell to mask the pain of moving, she shoved hard with her feet, trying to gain another few inches and felt another wash of fluid. She stared down at the ring of red spreading out from underneath her for a moment before shoving with her feet again, sliding nearly a foot from the force of her push.

So focused was she on moving she hadn't realized Tank had gone away until he was back, nudging her with his wide nose. "It's okay, baby," she tried to reassure him, hoping to reassure herself, too. He nudged her again, and this time dropped something into her lap. "No playing, honey. I need to get to the phone."

Looking down she expected to see an enormous rubber duckie, his favorite toy, instead seeing the familiar rectangular shape of the house phone. She looked at him and if she hadn't hurt so badly, would have laughed, the wrinkles in his forehead were so deep and pronounced they looked like chocolate valleys. "Good boy," she whispered, lifting the phone with one hand while propping herself up with the other. Thumb to the numbers, she dialed 911 and waited only a moment before the reassuring voice of the emergency operator came on the line.

"Nine-one-one, what is your emergency?"

Cadence screamed, and Tank barked once, then turned towards her room. The familiar sound of moving furniture sounded, then Cade quietened, and Sharon heard the creak of the crib as the big dog climbed in with his girl.

"Nine-one-one, can you tell me the nature of your emergency?"

Startled by the operator's repeat of the request, Sharon found her voice stolen by another contraction that she could only groan through. A minute, then another handful of seconds passed without it easing and she felt another gush of fluid between her legs, looking down to see this was clearer, red tinged as the amniotic fluid washed out of her in a wave. "I'm in labor. Something's wrong," she finally gritted out, and those words started the process of getting help on the way.

By the time the ambulance got there, Sharon was past any niceties and glad beyond words when she saw Goose's face hovering above hers. "Cadence," she gasped, cradling her belly. "The dog won't let anyone else get to Cade." She reached up, gripping his arm with all her might. "Call Gunny."

"I got it, honey," he reassured her and disappeared, another face popping into view, this of his partner Webber. She heard a thump and a growl, then Goose muttered something, and she was trying to focus on what was happening down the hallway while still attending to the questions Webber had for her about the contractions and bleeding.

"No, I don't know how far." She shook her head. "I had six days before my doctor was willing to induce, but I walked a lot today. I didn't want to do the meds. I'm so tired, Webby." Movement down the hall and she watched as Goose walked out of Cadence's bedroom with her in his arms, Tank the Larger pacing at his side, head angled up as he kept his eyes on his tiny charge. Relieved that Cadence was in safe hands, Sharon sagged backwards, barely getting to the floor before everything went dark.

***

Gunny

"Jesus, DeeDee," he complained, leaning back into the cushions of the couch in her office. "Why would you let that motherfucker back in here?" His callout had been to handle a customer who had barricaded himself in the women's dressing room. "And I'm still not sure why the service couldn't have handled it." When there was a meeting like tonight, Gunny had arranged with a local security firm to provide coverage at the businesses. The same one the Tridents used for their hockey games, and he'd never had an issue with them before.

"That was my call," DeeDee told him calmly. "When Brent locked the door, I wasn't sure all the girls were out. I knew he had a gun or thought he had one, anyway." Her voice turned disgusted. "Why do toy guns look so much like real ones?"

"Well, in your defense, he'd painted over the orange muzzle inset. Man's got a death wish or something." He sighed, rolling his neck. "I'm gonna head back to the clubhouse, see if there's anything left for me to do there." Pushing off the couch, he stood and stretched. "Man is slippery as a fuckin' eel," he muttered, feeling the pull of muscles he'd had to use to contain the offender.

Seated on his bike in the parking lot, he reached into his vest for his phone and came up empty, only then remembering he'd left the clubhouse in such a hurry he hadn't retrieved his phone from the locked box. "Fuck." He adjusted the choke and kicked the bike to life, sitting for a minute to let it warm up. Movement from the side surprised him, and his gun had already cleared the holster in the back waistband of his jeans before he got fully turned to face the threat.

DeeDee stood there, hands out to fend off a bullet she'd never see coming and Gunny winced to see how pale her face was. He killed the bike and heeled down the kickstand, standing up as he spoke over her babbled words, "Fuck, DeeDee. I didn't see you coming. Shit, honey, I'm sorry."

Time froze around him when what she was trying to say hit home. In one hand she clutched her jacket, and in the other a cell phone. He knew her mouth was still moving, still speaking, but he was stuck in a few seconds ago, hearing her say, "Sharon's at the hospital. Something's wrong."

***

Gunny deftly controlled the sideways slide as he whipped his bike around the final turn in the hospital's sweeping driveway. Hands clutched his belt on either side of his waist, and he slowed the smallest amount in deference to his passenger, but not much, knowing she could handle the ride. Skidding into a lined no-parking space near a light pole, he killed the bike and had it leaning on the kickstand in seconds, not waiting for DeeDee to dismount before he ran towards the ER entrance.

Glancing around, he was carried back in time more than a decade to the night he'd been called to the same hospital, meeting Ruby in the parking lot and consoling her about the death of Lockee and Winger, DeeDee's daughter and husband. Known as Melanie at the time, she'd been like a second daughter to the couple, Lockee her best friend. That was before Slate found her and renamed her, claiming her as his old lady, then as his wife. *Even at my worst, Melanie was never afraid of me. Like Sharon.*

There had to be a hundred motorcycles parked in scattered groups across the wide parking lot, some with men and women standing nearby or leaning against the bike. Every face he could see had the same wide-eyed stare, expressions carefully blank. They were here for him, here to support him, but the only news they had was bad. *Or old*, he held tight to that thought as he strode through the doors.

Mason stood in the middle of the room, flanked by Deke and Goose. Gunny took one look at the men's faces, then the blood on Goose's uniform registered and the room swung wildly around him, loud buzzing sounded in his ears. A painful pressure on his knees made him understand he'd gone down, legs swept out from under him with the fear he'd lost Sharon. DeeDee was on her knees beside him, Mason squatting a couple of feet away. Gradually he heard Deke's repeated words and swung his head to the side, seeing his best friend with one knee to the floor, hand hovering outstretched. "She's okay. Sharon's okay, Gunny. She's okay. The baby's okay."

Staring at Deke through a haze of tears, Gunny croaked out his question, asking for confirmation that the worst hadn't happened. "Sharon's okay? Kitten? The baby's okay, too?'

"Yeah, brother." Gunny sucked in a hard breath at the affirmation, feeling Deke's hand settle into place on the back of his neck. He pulled Gunny close as his head sunk down, chin resting on his chest while he tried to suck in enough air. Close to his ear, Deke spoke fast and low, imparting as much information as Gunny could take in. "It's all good, man. Goose delivered Kitten in the ambulance, and Bulldog's up with Sharon now. They're both okay. Gonna be okay. Sharon's good, and the baby's good, too. Bulldog's got her, and you know he does." Bulldog was a biker-friendly doc who had worked on Gunny overseas before settling here in Fort Wayne, giving up his native Toowoomba for the US after being discharged from the Australian Army.

"Cade," Gunny barked, head lifting suddenly. "Where's my little girl?"

Goose laughed softly, and Gunny looked to see him pointing towards a corner of the waiting room. "Mercy's got her. And that over there is the only wrinkle of the evening, apart from Sharon having to call emergency in the first place." Gunny turned his head to see Deke's woman, Mercy, bouncing a thank-God oblivious little Cadence on her knee, laughing down at the girl. Lying on the floor in front of the pair was a dark mountain, quiet and unmoving, head lifted alertly. Deke's little boy's head was resting on Tank's splayed paws, and Gunny knew the dog was staring at him over the sleeping toddler. "Hospital has a rule about pets, but I convinced them he was a companion dog and I failed to grab his vest. He wouldn't leave Cade's side. I tried to shut the door at your house, and he just grabbed the knob and opened it right back up. Climbed up in the ambulance like he was tired of waiting on my ass."

"Tank?" Shaking his head, he climbed to his feet, hating how unsteady he felt. "I gotta see Sharon. Brother." His voice broke and he clamped his lips

39

tightly, holding in the flood of pleas that tried to escape.

"I got you." Deke stood and nodded towards the bank of elevators.

The ride and rush through the corridors were a blur, and before he knew it, Gunny stood in the doorway of Sharon's room staring at her. Head tipped to the side, she was gazing down into the plastic-sided bassinette next to the bed, a smile on her too-pale face. While he watched, she settled down into the bed, tucking both hands under her cheek, eyes fixed on the sleeping infant.

With every breath, Gunny felt the darkness recede, the fear that had been pounding at him since hearing Goose's voice on DeeDee's phone. "Brother, get to the hospital now. Sharon's had the baby." Enough words to have him rocketing through the city streets, cursing the distance between Slinky's and the hospital.

As if she could feel his presence, Sharon's head rolled, turning so she looked at him. A broad smile split her face and she sighed, her happiness overcoming the exhaustion he saw lurking under the surface. "Hey, big guy."

"Hey, baby," he murmured in response, fingers tightening painfully on the edges of the doorframe.

"Kitten decided she didn't want to wait." Sharon lifted her hand towards him, fingers curled into her palm. "Come here."

His body surged forward, but his fingers kept their grip, holding him in place. "You're okay?" She nodded, stretching her fingers out. "You sure? Deke said Bulldog was here. Where'd he go?"

"Lane." Sharon looked at him steadily, knowing this was something he had to work through on his own. "I'm okay. Kitten's okay. Cade is okay." She swallowed, and her hand dropped an inch. "What I need to know is if you're okay." Tipping her head to the side, she looked away from him and towards the bassinette. "She's okay, honey. I promise."

He forced his cramping fingers to release and took the two strides to her side, catching her hand in his and bringing it to cover his heart as he bent to rest his forehead against hers. "You're okay."

"Yes."

"My Rose of Sharon." That was all he had to say because she knew what it meant to him. Her arms wrapped around his neck, holding tightly, holding on. "My life."

"Not going anywhere, Gunny. You're stuck with me."

"I love you, babe." He pushed a hand underneath her, feeling the solidness of her frame, the heat and weight of her body in his arm, cradling the back of her head with his other. "You're so fuckin' strong. I love you."

"Back atcha, Lane." Her arms squeezed, then released, and he pulled back, brushing across her lips with his, holding it to a light caress. When he pressed his forehead to hers again, she whispered, "Ready to meet your new daughter?"

"Yeah."

"Katherine Jacqueline Robinson, this big hulking guy is your daddy." Sharon was already talking as she pulled away, leaning towards the edge of the bed in a way that made his stomach clench. He reached out across her, hooked a finger in the corner of the bassinette and pulled, dragging the wheeled device closer. "Kitten, you and your sister have your work cut out for you. Daddy's going to be going all monster smash on any boys you bring home."

"Fuck, Shar, don't talk about her dating before I've even held her."

"Don't say the eff-word in front of our baby girl."

"Then don't push my buttons like you just were, babe."

Sharon grinned up at him, the tip of her tongue peeking out from between her teeth. "Okay. Now pick her up and hand her to me, baby's gotta eat because Momma started leaking about two seconds after you kissed me."

***

Gunny stretched, rolling slightly to the side, careful not to dislodge the sleeping Sharon from his chest. They were in the living room, Sharon pinned between him and the back of the couch. He twisted his neck, turning to look at the two girls sleeping, Cade in her playpen and a week-old Kitten in the portable bassinette, Tank the Larger laying on the floor between them.

After he'd crawled up in Sharon's bed at the hospital, holding her while she nursed their baby girl, she'd told him the story of what the dog had done. Kept her calm when she went into labor, brought her the telephone on command—something he still couldn't imagine—and then comforted Cade when the little girl needed him.

"Good dog, Tank," he murmured and watched as the dog's head came up, turning those intelligent eyes on where he lay with Sharon. A reassuring grumble from deep in the dog's chest sounded, and then Tank reclaimed his position, evidently satisfied with Gunny's grin in response.

Sharon had been shocked when Tank padded into the room alongside her brother, Jase, and DeeDee, a sleeping Cadence in Jase's arms. They had pulled Goose in so he could retell the tale of how Tank got to the hospital. Sharon listened, her eyes filling with tears as she ran her fingers over the dog's head, his chin propped on the mattress and eyes flickering between

Cade and Kitten. She'd turned her face against Gunny's chest and wept, overwhelmed by everything.

Later, when she and Kitten slept, Cade sent home with DeeDee and Jase, Gunny had sought out the Aussie doc. Deke had walked beside him towards the cafeteria, and Gunny hadn't been certain if it was in solidarity or to keep Gunny from killing the man if he found out anything he'd done while caring for a pregnant Sharon had put her at risk.

Turning his head now, he brushed her forehead with his lips, tightening his arm around her. It was nothing the doctors could have anticipated because Sharon hadn't had any of the symptoms of the condition—the placenta inside Sharon's womb had separated early. Too early. And with the child still inside, her uterus couldn't contract to control the bleeding. Too early for Kitten, too, and it was a wonder their daughter was okay.

Alternate scenarios kept playing out in his head, making him startle awake at night, and had him reaching out to make sure Sharon was there, warm and alive. Sharon could have died, bleeding out in the hallway of their home. She could have lived, but Kitten died, starved of oxygen and dying inside her mother's body. All the possible outcomes were bad, and the only one that mattered was what had happened. Sharon had been able to make the call in time. The ambulance was nearby, having just left the hospital after another run. It was Goose on the bus, so he knew all the players.

Gunny angled his head so he could see Tank the Larger again. Everything hinged on the dog. *Saved my family*. Tank's head lifted, and he shifted his hips to the side, rolling so he could see Gunny better. "Good dog." A reassuring thump of Tank's tail hit the floor twice. Then Gunny heard him groan and sigh as he laid down, stretching out his back and front feet to touch the girls' beds.

Chapter Three

Gunny

"Hey, brother," Gunny answered the phone with one hand, the other gripping a greasy rag. "How you doin', PBJ?"

A moment of silence, and then in a somber tone PBJ said, "Gonna be honest, man. I've been better."

Spine straightening, Gunny glanced around his garage, making sure everything was in its place. Rocky and Tank the Smaller lying in their beds along the wall, the door to the house closed, but the camera he'd installed showing a split screen of the kitchen/living room and the girls' room upstairs. Sharon was in the kitchen, bent over with her ass in the air, head in the refrigerator. He grinned, because if he were in there, she'd be bent over for a far different reason. His girls were sacked out in their beds: Cadence sprawled on her back, a toy in hand he knew from experience was a realistic-looking plastic mastiff; Katherine on her belly, head turned to the side, knees drawn under her.

All's well in my world, he thought, seeing Tank the Larger's head lift from his position on the rug between the girls' beds, eyes aimed not at the door, but at the camera by the ceiling. A chill rippled through his spine. *That dog.* Tank had proven himself to be near psychic, knowing just where to position himself to keep the girls from falling more than once.

"Tell me," he urged PBJ, letting his gaze drift back down to the carburetor he'd been working on before the phone rang.

"Brother." That sounded agonized, and Gunny was suddenly 100 percent focused on the voice coming through the phone. "I don't even know how to say this."

"Tell me." No longer a request, this was a demand, and PBJ gave way immediately.

"Breeder made contact. You remember when I was calling around after the bitch bailed on the dogs? None of the breeders knew of a mastiff in the area that fit Tank's description." Gunny's fingers twitched, cold, and he dropped the rag over the disassembled parts on the workbench.

"Yeah, I remember. Dog's mine." A growl echoed in the room, and he turned to see Tank standing in the open doorway, gaze pinning Gunny to the stool.

Sharon's laughter rolled through the door and her head appeared above the dog, hands reaching down to rub and tug at the loose skin on the sides of Tank's face. She looked up and whatever she saw on Gunny's face froze her in place for a moment. Then she was crossing the garage to circle his waist with her arms. "Don't care."

"Brother. You gotta hear the story."

"No." Nothing more, just a flat refusal was all he could grit out.

"Gunny, man. Dude's spent time in Walter Reed, and he's on his way here from rehab." That hit Gunny like a punch, because hearing that the military hospital was in play spoke to deployment, which might be the only reason a man should have left a dog like Tank behind. *Still.* "You need to hear the story."

"No, I don't. Don't fuckin' care, man. Dog. Is. *Mine.*" Sharon's arms convulsed, and he cradled the back of her head in the crook of his elbow, pulling her close, careful of the grease still on his hands. Heat pressed against his leg and he looked down to see Tank leaned into him, Tank the Smaller and Rocky now on their feet, anxious gazes locked to the trio by the bench.

"I'll come over."

"Not gonna fuckin' matter. Already told you." Gunny swallowed, because if PBJ was this adamant, then he knew the story would be a compelling one. "Had the dog nearly a fuckin' year. He's fuckin' mine."

"Let me come over."

"Come on, brother. Always welcome in my home." Sharon shivered, and he realized he was shouting. Gunny tried to dial it in a little, as much as he could. *Not takin' my dog. My girls' dog. He saved my family.* "But you ain't takin' my fuckin' dog." He threw the phone sidearm against the back of the workbench, not caring when the back popped free, battery and phone parting ways to fall in separate bins.

"Baby." Sharon's voice trembled nearly as much as she was.

"Not takin' him. Don't fuckin' care." He took a breath, then another, forcing as much air into his starving lungs as he could. "PBJ won't, and I know it. Just what he said hit hard."

The heat from beside him retreated, and a few seconds later, Cade's babbling sounded on the nursery monitor. Gaze to the screen showing the security camera feed, he watched Tank move through the living room and up the stairs, appearing a moment later in the girls' room. Front feet to the ottoman, the big dog shoved it next to Cade's crib, climbing over the side with a little hop. The dog lay down next to Gunny's daughter, careful of his feet and elbows, uncaring as Cade flung herself on top of him, face buried in the ruff of fur and skin behind his ear. Glancing across the space, Gunny saw Tank and Rocky were back on their beds, heads up and watchful.

"My fuckin' dog."

***

Gunny walked into Marie's and gave a low wave to Gypsy, who stood behind the cash register. The Rebel member managed the bar for the club but had been away for several weeks, so it was good to see him back in residence. Gunny reached across the bar to give him a warrior's shake, telling him, "Good to see you, brother. Was worried for a bit that the Down Under life would prove too attractive."

Gypsy released his hold on Gunny's wrist, smoothing his beard with the palm of a hand. Gunny was immediately on alert, because this was one of Gypsy's tells, a sign he was nervous. The ex-cop turned outlaw didn't get nervous often. "Yeah, good to see you too, Gunny. Glad to be back under familiar skies." He lifted his chin, indicating across the room, and Gunny used the mirrors to see where he indicated, there were two men seated at a booth near the back. "PBJ is already here. He, uh, said you were coming in."

"Said I'd be one pissed off motherfucker if this chat didn't go my way too, didn't he?" It wasn't a real question, but it still made Gunny angry that PBJ had resorted to older tactics to telegraph the possible fallout from today.

Lips pulling to the side, Gypsy grinned as he nodded. "Might have alluded to such a thing."

"Bastard." Gunny kept his tone conversational and tried to dredge up a return smile. "I'll go put him out of his misery." Already turning, he glanced back and asked, "Have one of the girls bring me an iced tea?"

"This really is about to get shitty, isn't it?" Gypsy acknowledged his order with a nod. "You got it."

PBJ was on the seat facing the room, the man who'd accompanied him here today sitting with his back to the room, but Gunny saw he was actively using the mirrored signs on the wall behind PBJ to watch his six. *Wonder how fresh he is stateside?* Striding up to the table, he glanced at the man, seeing scar tissue along his cheek and throat, then ignored him and stuck his hand out towards PBJ. "I'm here."

"So you are," PBJ returned, sliding to the edge of the seat and standing. He leaned in, pulling Gunny into a one-armed clinch, muttering in his ear, "Be easy, brother. He's good people."

Gunny stepped back as he turned to face the man who had also stood, finding himself in the unaccustomed position of looking up into someone's face. *Man that big, a mastiff fits him.* The skin on the man's neck pulled, strained tight and red where it disappeared into his army green tee. He stuck out a hand and Gunny reluctantly accepted the grip, impressed not that the man had strength, but that he didn't feel it necessary to clamp down and prove his manhood.

"Gunny," he grunted, releasing and stepping back, crossing his arms across his chest.

"Jock." That one-word introduction was followed by a slight headshake, and a correction, "Jacob. I'm Jake, I mean. Jacob Tinney."

Gunny stared up at the man, assessing. Now that he was looking for it, the tale-tell signs of PTSD were all right there. The slight tremor in his fingers as he fought not to match Gunny's aggressive stance, the beads of sweat that had popped up along the man's hairline, and even the inability to put a name to himself in a way that would stick. *Fuck. I don't want to like him.*

"Let's swap sides, man." Treading carefully, but hoping his instincts were right, Gunny swapped places, putting PBJ on the inside of the bench, and suffering through having his back to the room. Almost immediately the man relaxed slightly, pressing his palms flat on the table on either side of his ice water. "Jock." Deliberately Gunny used the first name provided, noting the slight jerk to the man's head when the word hit the air. "Tell me why you think this is your dog."

Jock's lips twitched sideways, one corner pulling up. "Other than the bitch who bailed on your man PBJ here was my little sister's best friend, who promised to pup sit when I needed a favor while I was deployed?"

Leaning forwards, Gunny rapped the table with his knuckles. "Yeah, other than that. Tell me what you think."

"I think my Neapolitan mastiff named Tank got tangled up in shit after my life fell in the crapper while I was in Afghanistan. He's a dark chocolate color, a big bastard of a dog who wouldn't hurt a fly. I think the bitch who was paid to watch him after my bitch of an ex dumped my ass, turned around and dumped his ass. I also think I'm lucky to have found where he landed." Jock stared at Gunny, breathing evenly but Gunny could see the pulse in his neck pounding. "Left and my wife was pregnant." Gunny went still at those words, afraid of what might come next. "Turned out the kid wasn't mine, and she knew that for truth soon as she had the boy. I'm kinda white—" Jock ran a hand through his light blond hair. "—and the boy wasn't."

"Shit, man. Sorry that happened to you." PBJ's mutter went unremarked by the two men locked in a stare down across the table.

"Tank's a good dog. I didn't want him to stay with her, not after everything happened the way it went down. My sister's friend looked like a good solution, seeing as I was nine goddamned time zones away when I got the divorce papers." Jock leaned in an inch. "Took me longer to get back than I expected."

"PBJ said you were in Reed." Gunny glanced to the side, seeing one of the waitresses with a tray of glasses. Water, tea, and beer. He waited until she'd deposited the drinks, then continued, "Said you came here straight from rehab. Where are you landing?"

Jock leaned back, shaking his head. "Not sure yet. I got nowhere to be right now. Due to Uncle Sam, my plans are…" He paused a moment and cut his eyes down to his hand and Gunny saw an indention on his ring finger. A leftover memento of a faithless marriage. "Somewhat flexible."

"You healthy?" Gunny's question had Jock's gaze whipping up, an aggressive jut to his jaw for the first time. "Got a doc to follow up with here? We got a bunch of ex-military guys in the MC. We all look out for each other." With every word, Jock's muscles lost rigidity until he was leaning back against the cushions behind him, the first time he'd relaxed like that. "Tell me what you need, man. Bust my hump tryin' to get it for you."

"Tell me about Tank." Voice hoarse with emotion, Jock dropped his gaze to the untouched glass of water slowly gathering runnels of condensation along the sides. "Tell me about my boy."

No reason to deny Tank was the man's dog, not with the breed and name lining up the way it was. Gunny settled back and lifted his tea, taking a long drink before launching into the story of how the mastiff had come to live in his home and be part of his family.

***

"Baby," Gunny shouted as soon as he was through the garage door. Jock was coming in ten minutes behind him by prearrangement, this not being something Gunny wanted to tell Sharon over the phone. "Where the fuck are you?"

Sounds from the backyard had him headed towards the sliding glass door off the kitchen. It was an unaccustomed warm day, and Sharon was on a blanket on the ground, Kitten beside her, kicking and flailing her way across the uneven surface. Cade was a few feet away lying on her back, staring up at the sky overhead. Tank the Larger was positioned between Gunny's family and the door and had lifted his head alertly. The ticking of toenails behind him warned of the approach of the other two dogs, and Gunny shifted to one side with the ease of long practice, letting the smaller dogs move around him and into the yard.

Tank didn't lose the alert look, though, not like he normally would have, and Gunny focused on him. Sharon stood, shaking her head back and forth. "No." The single word sounded like her heart was breaking, but for once, Gunny didn't rush to soothe her. He took two steps into the yard, gaze locked on Tank who had climbed to his feet, head up, scenting the air. Lumbering into a quick trot, he covered the ground to get to Gunny and then was on him, nose pressed to Gunny's right hand, snuffling and sniffing. He shook his big head and snorted, then hoovered Gunny's hand again, his big body nearly quivering with tension. Sharon's voice was small, quavering, "No, please."

"Smells the man on me. All I did was shake his hand and Tank smells him. Tell me you don't see this?" Gunny let the dog continue sniffing as he lifted his gaze to see tears trailing down Sharon's face. "Man's had a shit deal handed him, wife that cheated and let him believe her babe was his, then Dear Johned him while he was fuckin' deployed to the sandbox, honey. All he's got, and until yesterday, he didn't know he still had anything, but all he's got is Tank." He took two steps towards her, Tank moving with him, nose still avidly pressed to Gunny's flesh. "He's my fuckin' dog, and you know it. But Shar, he really isn't. Been on loan with us. Done us a hell of a turn."

"Saved my life," she whispered, holding her hands to the side, fingers spread. "Gunny, he saved Kitten."

"You think I don't know that? You think I don't thank God for this dog every single fuckin' day?" Tank carefully stepped around Kitten, leaving Gunny and pressing close to Sharon, offering comfort for a distress he recognized. "Look at him right now, lovin' on you like he is."

The roar of a bike's exhaust filled the air, followed by a quieter growl of a truck, and Gunny knew it would be PBJ and Jock. "Man's gonna come here. We'll see how things go. But—" He glanced down at his hand, covered in slobber. "—I'm bettin' the dog'll know the man."

"Hello, the house," PBJ called, as was the norm when a brother came over these days. Gunny turned to see him come through the sliding doors he'd left open, Jock following right behind him. There was a tentative, muffled groan from Tank the Larger, heard over the yapping barks of Tank and Rocky. Cade's babbling for her Unka Pee competed with a louder groan, and Gunny turned to see Tank already in motion, arrowing straight to the man who stood with his arms spread wide, not even having to call the dog.

Sharon stepped to Gunny's side, wrapping both her arms around his middle as they stood and watched the most joyous homecoming welcome Gunny had ever seen. Tank had his forepaws on Jock's shoulders, head buried under the man's chin and was leaping, his back legs gaining only four or five inches with each jump, but the excitement coming from the dog was palpable. His muscles quivered, tail snapping back and forth like a whip, vocalization finally happening as Tank found his voice, tinny yips and howls cut short when Jock went to a knee, wrapping his arms around Tank's torso, holding him close.

***

Sharon

"Yeah," Jock muttered as he shoved another forkful of mashed potatoes into his mouth, "Tank's been my bud since he was eight-weeks old. Me and him," Jock's hand dropped to caress Tank's head, propped on his thigh, "been through thick and thin."

Gunny answered, and PBJ pitched in a word or two, as did Deke, who'd come over for supper. She was glad they were supportive of Gunny, and from the look Deke had shot her way when he arrived, she knew they'd been expecting a different response about what was happening with the dog.

With one hand helping Cade navigate her meal, Sharon pushed food around her own plate with her other one, considering and discarding a series of ideas as too far-fetched. Listening to Jock talk about what had happened to him had been heartbreaking, but all she'd been able to really pick up out of the conversation was that he didn't have anywhere to take Tank. Didn't have anywhere to go, period, and the more she thought about it, the better her wild-haired idea sounded.

Gunny was responding to Jock as he did the men he'd been in the club with for years. He was open, unguarded, the way she loved to see him. *I need to keep this guy around for Lane.* Gunny still had issues with his PTSD, and she knew it would be a lifelong struggle for him, but the more she could surround him with good and decent people, the more at ease he became.

Cade dropped one hand down beside her highchair and seemed to realize for the first time that her constant companion wasn't nearby. Little head whipping back and forth, she used her little-girl sweet voice, the one that usually got her daddy to do whatever she wanted, and always called the dogs from wherever they were at the time. "Tank. 'Meer me. Tank." A minute went by without the dog moving. In fact, the only reaction Cade got was a fond glance from her father. Sharon smiled, knowing her daughter. A moment later Cade pulled in a deep breath, then slapped both palms against her chest and bellowed an unmistakable demand, "Tank. 'Meer me."

Sharon stared across the table as Jock's eyes widened, focused on tiny Cade. Then there were the shuffling heavy steps she expected as Tank moved around the table and to his little girl. Leaning against the legs of the highchair, Tank groaned when Cade's fingers found his ears, tugging and rolling them in a way he loved.

Gunny, seated as he was on Cade's other side, reached out and cradled the back of Cade's head, pulling her sideways so he could kiss the top of her head. For his efforts, he got nothing more than a sweet grin from their daughter as she crooned to Tank, "Good doggie, Tank."

Sharon glanced across the table and saw a look of clear longing on Jock's face. She knew he wanted what Gunny had, wanted what Tank had, even.

"I think you should stay here with us." Four wooden chairs around the kitchen table all creaked at the same time, as if every man had shifted in response to her words. "Give yourself time to get used to Tank again, and it will give my little girls time to get used to the idea that he's not a fixture in their lives." Jock stared at her, face pale, and Sharon wondered at that but then forged ahead. "I doubt any of these big, bad guys thought to tell you, but Tank saved my life." She pointed across the room to where Kitten dozed in the portable playpen. "Saved my daughter's life, too."

From the puzzled look on Jock's face, it was clear he didn't know the story, and Sharon turned to aim a glare at Gunny. He lifted both hands in an "I give up" pose, and she laughed. Looking at Jock, she saw genuine curiosity in his expression. "So, a bit ago, I was pregnant." Jock's eyes cut over to Kitten and Sharon nodded. "I was here at the house when I went into labor. Alone." Now Jock's gaze glanced towards Gunny, and Sharon was surprised at how his face had hardened. *He's getting pissed off on my behalf.*

"Things happened fast." She shook her head, the terror of that day having receded until this seemed just a story. "But something went wrong. I remember being so scared, so terrified because I was here alone and all of this was happening to me. Cade was here, and I was terrified for her. Tank—" She dropped her hand to caress the top of the dog's head, and he shifted, leaning against her hip. "—didn't just help keep me calm, he was like a labor coach. He knew when a contraction was coming and he kept crowding me, getting close, giving me something to hold onto. Poor guy—" She cupped his jaw, angling his head up so she could see those intelligent eyes. "—probably thought the crazy, yelling preggo lady was going to choke him, but he kept coming back for more."

She looked at Jock, knowing Gunny had gone still, too still, caught up in his own memories, but she needed to finish the story. "I was so scared. He kept checking on Cade, then coming back to me and one of those times I told him I needed the phone." She leaned forwards, one hand on the dog, one flattened to the table. "*He brought me the phone.*" Jock's head snapped back, and she nodded. "Yeah. Brought me the phone and then kept taking care of me and Cade.

When the ambulance got here, he was in Cade's room and let me tell you, it was a good thing the ambulance guy was a friend, because Tank wasn't about to let just anyone near his girl." She looked back down at Tank, smiling to see he'd shifted around so he was touching both Cade and her.

"All the way to the hospital he stayed by me. Then at the hospital, he stayed with Cade." She glanced at Gunny, seeing his hand still moving on their daughter's head, stroking her curls soothingly. Covering his hand with hers, she smiled at him. "And Kitten was born, alive and well, healthy and whole. All because my big guy brought home this big guy."

Pulling in a deep breath, she lifted her gaze to Jock, seeing wet in his eyes. "I'm not being a super-nice silly girl when I offer for you to stay here. You seem to need a place to just be who you are for a while, and I think it's great we can offer that. But this is me being a little bit selfish and wanting a few more days to tell the Tankster goodbye." Fingers working through the folds of skin under Tank's jaw, she felt as well as heard his groan. "Even Tank agrees!" Sharon smiled and waited, watching as Jock's eyes danced around the room, taking stock of Gunny's reaction along with the other two men. Jaw tight, he cut his gaze back to her and nodded once.

***

Gunny

He came awake, holding himself still and unmoving, listening in the dark to the sounds inside his house. All he heard were the normal environmental control noises of the air conditioner, the squeaky fan in the ductwork over the master bath that he kept reminding himself to oil, the quiet murmur of the baby monitor telling him all was well with his two girls. Nothing that would have pulled him from sleep.

Then he heard it. The tiniest gasp of an indrawn breath that hitched then cut off.

Gunny turned over in the bed, shifting Sharon from his shoulder and pressing one forearm into the mattress next to her head. Looming over her like this always emphasized the size difference between them, her so tiny her arms wouldn't wrap all the way around his waist. *Still, perfect for me.* "Baby," he murmured, leaning down to brush a kiss across her forehead, "why you cryin'?"

"I'm not crying." Her whisper was airy, breathy in a way that put the lie to her words and he grinned.

"Babe." Lips to her temple, he traced a kiss down her cheek to just behind her ear, pressing gently.

Stubborn, she angled her chin away, in one motion refusing to respond and yet responding, giving him the access he needed to get his mouth on her neck. Kissing softly, he worked down to her collarbone while his hand swept up her side, finding and cupping her breast. She shifted her lower body closer to him and he gave in to her silent demand, bringing his thigh up to rest on her legs, pinning her in place, his arm, leg, and body serving as a living frame.

"Mmmm," he murmured, feeling her arch up into his hand. "Jesus, baby."

"Gunny." The single word that slipped past her lips was filled with a longing he recognized, her desire painted on the air in a way that hardened his cock. Shifting against her rubbed the length of him across her hip, the head of his cock growing in a way that pushed his foreskin out of the way, sensitive flesh stroking across her heated skin.

"Gonna love on you, babe." That would be all the warning she needed, because every time they fell into each other's arms began the same way—words that had come to mean so much to both of them, echoing through the years back to the first time he'd been inside her after weeks of waiting.

As she did every time, that broad smile shone up at him. Even in the dark, he knew her eyes were dancing when she complained as if he'd been taking hours to get to this point. "Just love me already."

He bent to her, chasing the heat of her mouth with his lips, and as he kissed her, warned, "Don't think I'm forgetting my question, baby."

She gasped as he tugged the gusset of her panties out of the way, tracing the pads of his fingers through the wetness he found. "You—" She gasped again, hips moving up, responding to his touch. "—never forget anything."

"Damn straight," he told her, sliding down the bed, mouthing her breast through the nightshirt she wore. "Gonna eat you first, then fuck you."

"Okay," she agreed, and obligingly lifted her hips so he could divest her of the panties. Knowing what he wanted, knowing him so well, she bent at the waist and shucked off her shirt, falling to her back naked.

Afterwards, she cuddled into his side, hips angled so she could throw a leg across his thighs and he heard her sigh. "Tell me, babe."

Her voice was quiet and small when she said, "I should go clean up."

Gunny ran his palm down the sleek skin of her back, cupping her ass and squeezing before he trailed his fingers up her spine, shifting her hair off her shoulder so he could stroke the skin of her throat. When the doctor had given Sharon the all clear for sex after she'd had Kitten, Gunny made an appointment to go in and talk to the man by himself. Bulldog had told him the issues with Kitten's delivery were serious, but if he and Sharon wanted more babies, it was something they could watch out for differently. In other words, having another kid wasn't off the table.

He wanted another kid. Another two or three kids, in fact.

So from the time they started back with sex, he hadn't gloved up. Hadn't talked about it, because his Sharon wasn't dumb; she'd know it wasn't an oversight on his part. She also wasn't afraid to speak up, not anymore, and that meant if she didn't want to be pregnant, wasn't ready to add to their family, she would have said something or pressed a condom into his hand. She hadn't, and he hadn't, and now, he knew what had her crying.

"You're pregnant." Whispered softly, reverently, he waited a beat for her to respond, but she seemed frozen. "Tits are sensitive as hell, like you always get. I saw you ain't got any kind of appetite, and baby,"—he grinned into the darkness—"you were hot for me tonight."

"I'm always hot for you." She rolled, burying her face against his abs. He stroked down her back, and back up, again and again, giving her time to put her words together. "What if—"

"Nothing bad is going to happen to you."

"You can't know that." Her hair moved across his skin, delicate traces of a barely-there touch. "I'm not worried about me, anyway. What if something happens to the baby?"

"You love me?" She jolted in surprise at his question, then nodded, her hair again dragging across his skin. "And I love you. Nothing is going to happen, Shar."

"You can't know that." She fell back on the same argument, and while she was right, she was also wrong.

"I can know. Big man upstairs isn't going to put me through hell on earth and then give me an angel only to take any part of her shine away." He wrapped his arm around her, pulling her tight to his side, lifting her jaw with a curled knuckle. "You're my Rose of Sharon. My shining star. You—" He bent and kissed her forehead, then her nose. "—are my reward for coming out the other side." He brushed his lips across her forehead again, holding her close. "How far, baby?"

"Just a few weeks." She stretched up, and he tipped his chin, letting her capture his mouth. She pulled back and whispered, "Barely even preggers."

"Bullshit."

"What? No, it's just I'm barely even pregnant." Rolling her eyes, she shook her head as he laughed.

"Sharon, you can't be just a little bit pregnant. It's one of those all-in things. You either aren't—" He paused, waiting, and she shook her head. "—or you are." She nodded. "Bulldog, first thing tomorrow." She nodded again, settling in beside him. "Love you, Sharon."

"Love you, too, big guy."

***

Gunny startled awake, hyperaware of every current of air moving through the room. Sharon was sleeping deeply. Just over eight weeks pregnant, her tummy was still tender, and without eating like she should while chasing after two kids, she was exhausted each night when she fell into bed. Something that made him feel guilty and worry, but *God*, the end result would be so worth it. Still, whatever woke him wasn't her.

A muffled sound from the hallway had him moving towards the door, 9mm in hand. As he neared the door, he heard the sound again, recognizing it as Tank the Larger's distinctive deep growl. Gunny's eyes darted around the darkened room, verifying nothing was amiss. Then he palmed the doorknob, holding it steady as he slowly turned it and drew it open just a crack.

Jock stood near the top of the stairs, facing towards the girls' bedroom, fingers tearing through his hair. The lines of his body screamed tension, and Gunny was about a half a second from tackling the man when a shadow near the girls' doorway moved, resolving into the mastiff. For once Tank's footfalls were soundless, but as the dog advanced towards Jock, that determined warning growl came from deep in his chest again. Gunny didn't have to see the dog to know he was serious, the noise rolling from the dog's throat held a threatening edge.

Easing the door closed behind him, putting a barrier between whatever was about to happen and Sharon, Gunny considered the situation for a moment. Jock was between him and his girls, but Tank was between Jock and the girls, and regardless of who the man was to the dog, Tank didn't seem to be in the mood to back down. Gunny waited a moment, then another, but Jock didn't move. Like a statue, the man stood so still Gunny wasn't certain he was breathing. *Dead man walking*. That thought sent a chill down his spine. *I remember those days*. Jock didn't acknowledge anything, not even the dog standing only feet away. *Gotta be me*. "Jock," he called softly, unsure at this point if the man was sleepwalking—not something Gunny had seen evidence of in the weeks he'd lived with them—or if he were caught in the grip of something more powerful than sleep. "Jock, man. You okay?"

No reaction, and until Tank's head shifted position slightly, Gunny wasn't certain he'd spoken aloud. "Jock," slightly louder, he was still hesitant about approaching, and then it happened. With an abrupt movement that had Gunny leveling the gun, Jock twisted to face him, and Gunny saw the tortured expression on his face. Folding at the hips and knees, Jock went to the floor, Tank barking at him, a massive and deafening roar of a sound. Belly to the floor, Jock wrapped his arms around his head, holding tight, hands curved as if they were still cupping a gunstock. Tank barked again, and Jock shrieked in response, the noise so loud Gunny felt it up through his bare feet on the wooden floor. It was a moment or two before he made out the words, and that only barely over the sudden screams of his daughters, frightened out of sleep by the ruckus.

"They're all dead." Those words, in various configurations, at times spliced together with a fusillade of names. Call names for a team that never left the patch of sand where Jock had been injured.

Gunny had talked about his own experience over backyard beers one night, the simple miracle of open sky and lightning bugs framed by the background sounds of Sharon getting the two girls ready for bed. Talked about the ambush that took his team, admitting his own feelings of culpability because of the bitch he'd bedded. Words had rolled out of him, covering the time spent in the desert alone, wounded and terrified. How he'd gotten back to Camp Chesty, taking a chance on a stranger who turned into a savior. Jock had listened, nodding his head at times, wincing at things that might have cut a little deep. Listened, but didn't offer his own story.

Knowing there was one, Gunny had Myron dig deep, and what he'd found had been horribly familiar. An isolated convoy decimated by hell raining down from the hillside, help five minutes too far away, explosions and bloody wounds and death everywhere. Twenty-two men rolled out from behind the wire on that patrol, and twenty-one came back in body bags. Jock had been pinned by flaming debris, suffering burns over much of his body. The scars Gunny had seen above the collar of his shirt were the least of them, and he knew from the grapevine that the rehab place in San Antonio where Jock spent time usually only accepted the worst cases.

Gunny heard the handle of his bedroom door jiggle, and before Sharon could open it, he called out softly, "No, baby. Stay inside. I got this. Girls are fine." The last thing he wanted was to have her injected into the scene. She'd be warped because of Jock being on the floor and without knowing what the guy's triggers were, Gunny was wary of approaching the guy himself, forget Shar who weighed a buck five on a pregnant day.

"Okay." There was a distinct tremor in her voice but, *thank God,* she trusted him.

Fuck. Staying out of reach, he knelt and started talking. Easy conversation, he kept to areas that would help pull Jock back into now, extending topics from last night's dinner, spinning stories out and then pulling back to cover ground a second, then a third time. Jock's only reaction was a flinch when Tank eased to the floor, lying alertly, propped on his elbows.

Jock rocked back and forth on his elbows, wiggling away from the door and towards the stairs. Tank groaned and Jock stopped. They stayed like that for minutes, Gunny talking and Jock and Tank stock still as the girls' cries slowed and stopped, trailing off as they slipped back into a doze and then sleep.

Finally, fucking finally, he heard Jock sigh. It sounded like the weight of the world was still on the man. Gunny shifted from his awkward position on his knees and sat on his ass, leaning against the wall. He held out a hand and Tank's head swung, looking at him. Gunny curled his fingers a couple of times, silently calling the dog, then pointed at Jock. Tank stared at him for a moment, then looked over his shoulder towards the girls' door before returning his gaze pointedly to Gunny. This is on you if it goes bad, he seemed to be saying, and Gunny nodded.

Jock tensed when Tank lumbered to his feet and shook, the tags on his collar jingling. Then Gunny saw that tension flowing away as the dog settled back to the floor pressed tightly along Jock's side. He gave it a minute, then queried quietly, "You back, man?"

Silence for a moment, then Jock spoke, his voice grating over too-dry vocal cords, sounding as painful as Gunny knew it had to feel. "Yeah." Tank moved his head, twisting sideways to reach Jock's hand, his tongue slowly licking the back. "Good boy, Tank." Tank shook his head, tags jingling again. "Yeah, you are. Don't argue, asshole." Tank groaned and twisted more, resting his massive head across Jock's shoulders, his eyes trained on Gunny. The man's pain was echoed in the dog's eyes, and Gunny swallowed hard.

"Brother." The title felt right to Gunny, felt like he and Jock had survived something together right here in this hallway. "You got some shit in your head."

"Yeah." Jock sighed, and Tank's head went up and down with the movement. "I don't know why I'm up here." Another sigh, Tank's eyes still fixed on Gunny. "I got no reason to be up here by your family. Fuck." Jock turned his head away, burying his face into Tank's neck. "I got no reason to be here at all."

"You believe in fate, brother?" Gunny did. He'd lived through too much to think lives connected by chance. If he'd not taken the job with the city, he would have never met Deke. Not meeting Deke meant no Rebels. No Rebels meant no Sharon, no babies. "I think your dog wound up with me so we'd meet." Tank's eyebrows went up, his nose wrinkling. "Not sayin' your life falling to shit is so you can say you know me, but I think me knowing you was a done deal once your shit hit the fan. I've been where you are. Been around that block so many fuckin' times, I know where all the cracks are. I've been you, brother. And I think you came to me because I can help."

"What the fuck am I supposed to do, man?" Muffled against Tank's fur, the tears were thick in Jock's voice. "I'm not...fuck. I'm not useful. I got no job, got no woman. Fuck. Got nothing to hold on for except...all I could think of was finding Tank. Kept my finger off the trigger, because I had to know where my dog was."

"You held on, brother. Held on and found him."

"Yeah, but now what the fuck do I do? I can't even take care of him." Jock slipped sideways, curling around Tank and the dog let him, adjusting his position to stay in contact while his gaze never left Gunny. Find a way to fix this, he seemed to be saying.

"You don't do this alone. That's the first thing you have to understand. You try to do it on your own, and you'll fail. It's too big, brother. Give some of it to me. Let me help you get what you need to find your way out the other side of the valley." Gunny slid close, resting one hand on Jock's shoulder, feeling the heated gusts of Tank's breaths rolling across his wrist. Jock was shaking, shivering, his body throwing off the adrenaline in a way that would make him feel weak. Gunny knew how it felt because he'd been caught up in this more than once. "Let me help you." He pressed hard, pushing to hold Jock down, easing the quivering of muscles causing him to jerk in place. "I got a doc who can be here in twenty minutes, you greenlight me to call. He's good, brother. No bullshit. He's the thing that helped me find my way back when I nearly lost myself after I met Sharon."

"What?" The shock in Jock's voice was sharp, biting. "I thought..."

"Fuck, no. Love of a good woman helped, but in some ways"—he wasn't saying anything she didn't already know, so Gunny didn't worry about hurting her if she was still listening—"it made things harder for a while. I kept flashing, and then I'd freak because what if I hurt her? What if I hurt my soulmate? What if the things in my fucked-up head got twisted around and I put my hands on her? Too precious for words that woman, and I couldn't stand the idea, but once it started, it burrowed deep. So deep I wasn't sure I'd ever dig it out. This doc, the one I mentioned, he helped me sort out my head."

"He pushes drugs, doesn't he? They all do." Jock sounded disbelieving, but that was threaded through with hope.

"Drugs have a place, brother. They can. But if it's a no-fly for you, then he'll work with what you give him. He's not an idiot, though, so if he says they can help, he's probably right. They're a tool, just like anything else." Tank sighed, his head rocking to the side as his eyes closed, finally, and Gunny knew it was because he could feel Jock relaxing. "We can't turn our backs on help, brother. Let me make the call."

"I could have hurt your girls." Jock's voice was thin as he spoke the words, the man's worst fear laid bare for Gunny's ears.

"Nope. Tank had your back, brother. He wasn't gonna let you get close to doing anything you couldn't come back from." *Thank you, God.*

Chapter Four

He'd been here so often, Gunny didn't even flinch when the sliding doors of the VA hospital closed behind him, shutting out the glare of the late summer sun along with the fresh air. What he strode through now were sluggish currents of stale, medicinal-tinged drafts, each breath seeming to amplify the message that here was where people without hope came. *But hope finds 'em, regardless.* He angled across the lobby towards the small hallway leading to the talking doc's office, a route learned years ago, reinforced by these past six weeks of visiting Jock as often as he could.

The doc had phoned this morning, talking through the process of releasing Jock from the inpatient ward where he'd been staying. As Gunny had promised, it was his own choice that put him on that ward. And now, it would be a combination of recommendation from the doc and Jock's decision that would put him back on the outside.

Having only seen the process from inside his own head, Gunny wasn't certain what his role would be today and for the weeks to come. Another promise to Jock, he'd have a place to land, no matter what. Rounding the corner, he saw the doc's office door was partly open, a murmur of voices coming from inside. He knocked and within a moment was invited to, "Come on in. The door's always open."

Inside, Jock sat on the edge of a chair he'd pulled up to the desk that took up so much of the space in the room. He looked up at Gunny and it was with relief that Gunny saw much of the tension Jock had still carried even a couple of weeks ago had melted away. A genuine smile lit his face, his cheeks lifting and crinkling his eyes. *Almost looks like a different person.*

"Hey," Jock said as he stood, hand thrust out for a wrist clasp from Gunny. "Doc laid everything out. Appreciate everything you're doing for me, man."

"No worries, brothers stand together." There was a squeak from the doc's chair, and Gunny turned to see he'd risen to his feet, assessing gaze moving between the two men. "We good, Doc?"

"Yes. Everything's sorted from my end of things."

Jock interrupted, bringing Gunny's attention back to him. "You sure about this? It's…" Some of the ease went out of the man's expression, his features taking on a drawn aspect. "It's a lot, man."

Gunny leaned in, thudding Jock's shoulder with each word as he repeated himself. "Brothers stand together."

It was quiet in the truck on their drive back to Gunny's place, Jock declining any fast food to hold him over until dinnertime. The miles rolled past and Gunny let his mind wander to how things could have been different for him. *If I hadn't found Shar in time*. "Need to warn you, having some friends over. You've met some of 'em, PBJ for sure, and I think you met Deke in the garage one day." From the corner of his eye, he saw Jock nod. "Yeah, thought so. Anyway, they're coming over, poker night. Sharon will probably stay in the living room with the kids, and we'll need you at the table."

"Nah." Jock's refusal seemed automatic, not something he had to think about. Gunny knew how that was, too.

"Yeah, you ain't holin' up in no fuckin' bedroom while there's poker to be played. Mason, the head honcho of the MC is gonna be there, and I already told him you're playin'." He grinned out the windshield, seeing his exit approaching. "Don't make me out a liar, brother."

There was humor in Jock's voice when he asked, "And if I say I'm not feelin' it?"

"Draggin' your ass out there anyway, turd." Gunny sucked in a breath, feeling his shoulders lower a couple of inches, glad Jock was comfortable enough to joke.

"Thought you called me brother?" Gunny glanced over to see Jock turning to look out the window, a smile on his face.

"I do, except when you're actin' like a turd. Then I call a turd a turd." He took the upcoming exit, aiming the truck home. "Don't mean you're not my brother. Just that, in that moment, you're also a turd."

"Glad we clarified that, then." Jock chuckled and Gunny grinned.

"Good deal."

At the house, they walked into chaos that made Gunny's grin widen even more. Cade and Kitten were in high chairs drawn up to the kitchen table, a mixture of singing and screaming coming from them. While their hands and faces were messy, the floor around the chairs was conspicuously clean. The dogs were ranged on either side of the girls as they walked in, and when Tank the Larger abandoned his post to pad quickly over to Jock, he heard the man whisper, "Good boy."

Sharon turned from her position in front of the stovetop and Gunny frowned to see lines of strain drawn on her pale face. It felt like this pregnancy was taking more out of her than the previous two. From the number of pots and pans, she was working on supper for the grownups. *One thing I can take off her plate.* "Cop a squat, Momma. I got this." He turned to tell Jock it wouldn't be long before dinner and paused, holding still as he took in the scene. Jock had seated himself in the chair that separated the two girls and had scattered cereal on Cade's tray. He had a jar of baby food in one hand, a spoon in the other, and had pushed his face close enough to Kitten's that she'd latched onto his hair with one food-smeared hand.

"Yeah, Momma," Jock cooed, his attention on Kitten's mouth as he plied her with a spoonful of food. "We got this."

Sharon smiled up at Gunny, holding her hands up in surrender and pushed close, lifting her face for a kiss. The slight swell of her belly pushed against him when he wrapped his arms around her, pulling her close. "Thank you," she whispered, lips still pressed to his. "I'm just so tired today."

"Then go nap," he told her in a return whisper. "I'll wake you with a plate."

She leaned against him, cheek to his chest and told Jock, "Welcome home." Gunny watched as Jock's eyes flickered, gaze darting first to Gunny's face, then to Sharon's, his head tipped to the side as Kitten tried to pull his hair to her mouth. "Thanks for helping with the girls."

"No problem." Reaching up, Jock extricated himself from Kitten's grip, and she turned immediately to slapping at her tray, making a racket. "Gunny called me a turd. I figure I'm family now."

"Gunny!" Sharon leaned back, frowning up at him. "We don't call people turds."

Chuckling, Gunny reached around her to pick up the spatula to stir the contents of the skillet. Narrow strips of vegetables sizzled in oil, and he peeked under the lid of a saucepan, seeing rice through the steam. "Baby." He looked into another pan and frowned. Nipples in boiling water. *Not food.* "Shar, did you cook all the veggies I cut up for your snacks?"

She pulled out of his arms and backed away a couple of steps. "Maybe."

"Did you get to the store today?" She shook her head. "Did you eat lunch?" Wrinkling her nose, she shook her head again. "Baby."

"I know. I'm just tired." Chewing on her lip, Sharon eyed him cautiously. "I called Bulldog. He said not to worry."

"Then don't worry." Gunny turned to face the pots and pans, hiding an expression he knew held fear, the memory of Goose standing in the ER with Sharon's blood on his shirt rushing at him out of a dark tunnel. "Go lay down." Sharon's footsteps retreated, echoing through the living room and then passing up the staircase. As if he were returned to the moment, Gunny was breathing in the biting, astringent scent of the ER, felt again the chill of the tile under his knees as he knelt and waited to learn if his life had been ripped apart. Reaching out blindly, his hand knocked against a hot pan, and he jerked back with a curse, hearing water sizzling as the pan overturned. "*Fuck!*" Hands to the counter on either side of the stove, he stared down at the liquid covering the surface, nipples for Kitten's bottles scattered next to the pot lying on its side. "Fucking shit."

"Dude, you're scaring the kids." Jock's calm voice broke the silence and Gunny jolted in place, pulled from his memories. He reached out, grabbed the pan's handle and set it to the side, plucking the nipples from the remaining water, dropping them back into the pan. "So, shit still gets to you, huh?"

"Doc's got a word for it. Said once you've dealt with it, it's like PTSD becomes a risk factor." Spatula in hand, he turned to see Cade studying him, her hand turned sideways as she tried to shove a piece of cereal into her mouth. "Hey, baby girl. How's Daddy's girl?" She dropped her hand and squinted at him, eyes nearly disappearing behind her lids. Then she opened them wide, a smile breaking across her face. "There's my girlie. Love you, Cade."

"Bu bye," she called, looking at the hand turned to wave at herself. Still waving, she refocused, grinning up at him. "Bu bye."

"Hello," Jock chuckled, and Cade whipped her head to stare at him. He waved at her and repeated himself, "Hello."

"Bu bye." Now she was scowling at Jock.

"Hello."

"Bu bye."

 "Hello."

"No 'lo. Bu bye."

"Brother, she can do that all day long." Gunny turned off the burner under the rice, stirring the skillet of veggies again before opening the refrigerator. He pulled out a half-eaten rotisserie chicken and began slicing thin pieces of meat, adding them to the skillet. "Chicken stir fry."

"Hello." Jock chuckled as Cade scowled again, her repeated "Bu bye" rumbling underneath his words. "Sounds good."

Gunny was outside after cleaning up from dinner, watching the dogs play carefully around the girls in the backyard. Sharon had dozed off after eating, and his guests wouldn't show up for another hour, just enough time to exhaust the kids so they'd sleep well, bathe them, and tuck them into bed. He heard the scuff of shoe leather on the cement and didn't have to look to know who it was, Tank the Larger's head had come up, and his eyes were focused behind Gunny with an intensity he reserved for three people: Cadence, Kitten, and Jock.

"Folks'll be here in an hour. You can have my chair. Gonna let the puddle ducks play in the tub for a bit.

PBJ's bringin' beer since Shar didn't get to hit the store today." He passed along this info without turning, eyes on Tank where he lay between the girls and the yard's back gate. *He's always on guard.* "Come here, baby girl." He stood, stretching before he walked to where Cade was already reaching high, wanting to be picked up.

"I can carry Kitten if you want." Gunny nodded, swung around and watched as Jock tenderly gathered the girl, Tank stood next to Jock's feet and watched attentively. "She's a year old? Turned while I was in VA, right?" Gunny swallowed hard, hearing the wistful tone in the man's voice. He thought Jock probably wouldn't ever be past the betrayal his wife had done, every milestone seen in another child a reminder of how things wouldn't be going for him. "Cade is two?"

"Just over two, yeah. There're thirteen months between my girls." With skill born of long practice, Gunny avoided stepping on any dog toes as he moved through the house and up the stairs. "Our bun will be almost eighteen months younger than Kitten. Seems a good spread."

"Boy or girl?" Gunny settled Cade in the tub, adjusting the flow and temp of the water. He reached up, taking Kitten from Jock's arms.

"Don't know yet. Not sure Shar wants to know with this one. She told me three women in a house is plenty, I'm pretty sure she's afraid it's another girl." He settled Kitten into the seat that had a permanent place in the tub, grinning as she squealed and kicked her feet, splashing herself in the process.

"Towels are on the seat. I'll grab pj's and lay them out." Jock walked out, moving quietly.

Heat crowded Gunny's back, and he twisted to see Tank still working to wedge himself into the small room, pressed tight to Gunny and facing the door. He frowned, considering the dog's behavior. In the first moments after he and Jock walked in, Tank had gone to the man and stuck with him for a few minutes before resuming his position near Cade and Kitten. But Jock had been right there, so that made sense. In the yard, the dog had stayed with the girls, and just now, had done the same. He remembered Tank's violent reaction to Jock the night everything fell apart and felt a curl of fear in his gut.

The doorbell rang and Tank the Smaller along with Rocky scrambled down the stairs, throwing themselves against the door as Gunny heard PBJ's voice, "Hello, the house."

"Hey," he called, "I'm upstairs with the girls. Go ahead and setup in the kitchen, brother. I'll be down directly." Surprised when footsteps moved up the stairs, he felt a rumble from Tank as he leaned back to look down the hallway. "Mason, brother." The rumble grew into a growl, and Mason halted a few steps back from the open doorway. "Tank, stand down. This is Mason." Another grumbling growl and then Tank settled on his haunches, sitting behind Gunny. "Jesus, stop leaning, asshole." Gunny shoved an elbow behind himself, trying to lever the dog off his back. "Tank, down." With a groaning complaint, Tank settled to the floor. "Come on in, Mason. He's a tad bit protective of the girls."

"Like their daddy is, no doubt." Mason stood next to the tub and grinned down, leaning a shoulder against the wall. "I needed to come see my boy's potential old ladies, brother. Never know how early to start matchmaking."

Gunny grinned, his hand cradling Cade's skull as she rolled over, a toy to her mouth, eyes fixed on Mason in a dark study. "Thought you'd paired Gar-boy with Faynez?"

Mason made a noise, clucking with his tongue and Cade rewarded his efforts with a broad grin before waving and shouting, "Bu bye."

Chuckling, Mason crouched down and had just started to reach out to take Cade's hand when Tank growled, the low, menacing sound echoing in the room. Gunny looked over to see Mason frozen in place, eyes on the dog, and the dog was staring at the doorway where Jock had stopped. "Tank," Jock scolded, "be quiet. Come." Heaving to his feet, the dog stalked on stiff legs towards the door, not even sparing a glance at Mason. "We'll be downstairs. Hi." He waved at Mason. "I'm Jock."

"Mason." Gunny watched, puzzled, as Mason remained crouched down, not even offering his hand to Jock. His tone was cautious and cold when he said,

"We'll be down in a bit. PBJ and Deke are stockin' the fridge. Could use a hand, I suspect." Kitten splashing pulled Gunny's attention back to the tub where Cade was once again chewing on a toy, staring at Mason. Gunny finished bathing the girls in silence and handed a towel-wrapped Cade to Mason, carrying Kitten to the girls' room. "You're watchful of him, right?" Mason's question seemed to come out of left field, and Gunny shifted on his feet, uncomfortable with what seemed to be an instant dislike between the two men. "Not sayin' he's a bad dude, just...be watchful, yeah?"

"He's had a shit hand, Mason." Gunny rested a hand on Cadence's back, watching as she snuggled into the mattress, hand wrapped tightly around her mastiff toy.

"Don't doubt it. Been read in on what went down with him." Mason walked soundlessly to the door and stood, waiting. "Also been read in on what went down in your house, brother. I get that you feel for him. I do. Just, be watchful."

"He reminds me of me." He stroked up and down Cade's back, soothing her gently as she found her way into sleep. "Man's worth the effort."

"I'll accept that." Gunny looked up to see Mason's gaze fixed on Kitten, one corner of his mouth curling up. "She's pretty, Lane. You made some beautiful children with Sharon."

"Thank God they take after their momma." He dimmed the lights, turning on the monitor before pulling the door closed. "Imagine if she had to look at two of me."

"The horror. Still, I think Shar would manage okay." Mason chuckled. "Let's go play some poker."

He lifted his chin, grinning. "Yeah, let's see if you can win somethin' off me."

Four hours later, Gunny was feeling less generous towards Mason. "Jesus, Prez. Fold. I got diapers to buy, brother." He tossed his cards on the table and pushed backwards.

"Me, too, brother." Mason chuckled. "My last hand. If I don't get home before daylight, I turn into a mean pumpkin."

Jock yawned and pushed his chair back. After a final glance at his cards, he lay them on the edge of the table. "Fold."

The hand continued for a few minutes, with Mason coming out the winner again. Some good-natured grumbling from PBJ and Deke, then they were on their way. Mason followed Gunny out the sliding glass doors with the dogs, standing with feet spread wide, looking up at the sky. "I miss this."

"What?" Gunny kept his eyes on the white flag of Rocky's tail. The terrier had been trying to dig out from under the fence to get into the fields surrounding the house, no doubt because he smelled gophers or some other critters. As late as it was, Gunny had no interest in chasing the dog tonight.

"Seein' the sky like this." Mason sighed. "My house is nice, don't get me wrong, but it's surrounded by people and people bring lights and noise. Here..." He sighed again. "It's nice. Quiet. And you can see the stars. Good place, brother." A footstep behind them announced Jock's arrival outside.

"Myron did good." Gunny passed off any credit for finding the house to where it was due, because all he'd done was give Myron a single item on a list of must-haves: No people. "He was over here last week flying that fuckin' drone you bought him."

Mason laughed, still staring up at the sky. "Smartest thing I ever did was patch that bastard."

"What, uh...what do you look for in a patch member?" Jock's voice was quiet, his tone solemn, fitting when asking what might be a life-changing question.

Gunny grinned, keeping his focus on Rocky's tail out near the back corner of the yard. He'd let Mason field that one. He heard Tank the Larger growl and a complaining yip from Rocky, then watched as all three dogs appeared at the edge of the light. *Good dog*.

"Big dog." Mason's words might have been aimed at Tank, but Gunny knew better. Jock made a questioning noise, and Mason snorted a laugh. "That's what we...I want. I have hundreds of members, and each one has been chosen for what they can bring the brotherhood. Here, in Fort Wayne? I'm looking for big dogs, men who can hang, no matter what the challenge thrown at the club. We've got shit on the horizon, and I need to have men I can trust in place to deal with whatever comes. So, in a word, I'm lookin' for big dogs to run with the rest of us, not stay on the porch."

"What does it take to run with your big dogs?" Jock sounded like this was a more than casual curiosity, and Gunny suspected it was a natural progression, given the weeks he'd had to study the brotherhood Gunny enjoyed with the members.

"First we get to know you, and vice versa. It's called the hangaround time, and it's kinda what you were doing tonight. You wanna explore what you see, then we have different conversations." Mason shifted to the side, turning to face the house, including Jock in their circle. "We get a lot of hangarounds. Lotta different reasons. Men who like the idea of power, because this patch offers that. People who want respect, because this patch brings that to the table in a big way."

Gunny interjected because he thought he knew where Jock was coming from, maybe more than Jock did. "We also get a lot of men who need to belong. It's a brotherhood, and when you wear the patch, you are guaranteed only one thing. Every man who also bears the burden of the patch has your back. It's both like and unlike the military in that respect. You walk into a bar with a member, and you know he's got your six. And you know he's depending on you to have his." He shrugged, dropping a hand to rub gently at the folds of skin behind the mastiff's ears. "Within the club, there are friendships, like me and Deke, PBJ, and even this fuckin' reprobate here." He tipped his head towards Mason, drawing a grin from his friend's face. "So I'd expect it from them. Brotherhood means that even members I don't know and never met would have my back."

"Military makes sure you know how to depend on a team." Jock nodded and turned to look beyond Mason, into the darkness. "It's not a team if that trust doesn't go both ways. Food for thought, thanks, Mason."

"Anytime." Mason moved, gripping Jock's shoulder. "Good to meet you, man. Heard good things about you." Turning to face Gunny, Mason reached out, pulling him into a one-armed clinch, pounding his back as he said softly, "I was wrong."

"Fucker." Gunny grinned and released his hold. "I'll be in the garage tomorrow, got a call for a custom build, want to go over things with Bear."

"Can't wait." Mason padded towards the house, one hand held up in farewell.

***

Jock

He stood in the room where he'd been staying, turning in a slow circle, taking in the emptiness surrounding him. *It's time.* Bending, he gripped the strap on his duffel and slung it over his shoulder. In the two weeks since he'd gotten out of the VA, things had gone from moving slow as molasses on a cold day to faster than light. On the second day, he'd gone with Gunny to the club's garage and met a dozen members. Of them, he'd hit it off with a dude named Domino, Deke's older brother. The man was struggling against the perception that since he was a former cop, he was a narc, but Jock saw something deeper in him. Domino's girlfriend was out of town for a few weeks, and he'd offered his second bedroom as a place to stay while Jock looked for an apartment of his own. It was his house, so could be as dog-friendly as Jock needed, which meant Tank was coming with him.

Gunny hadn't argued, not that he could; they'd established early on that Jock was Tank's owner. Sharon hadn't argued either, at least not verbally, but Jock had seen her sad eyes following the mastiff around the house for the past week. He knew the story, had heard it a dozen times, not just how his dog had wound up with such awesome people, but what Tank had done for her and Kitten. That day at the garage he'd listened to each man in turn as they approached him with their version of how Tank had gotten to the hospital, sticking close as glue to Cade until Gunny got there.

With a last look around the room, he strode out, heading towards the front door. Tank had been pacing back and forth between the bedroom and kitchen for the past hour, knowing something was changing with Jock, but wanting to be close to where Sharon was feeding the girls. Jock stood in the doorway, fingers nervously tracing the edge of the duffel's strap, waiting for Sharon to look up. When she did, he winced, because her eyes were rimmed with red, signs of tear tracks on her face.

Tank lifted his head and stared at Jock, then pushed to a seated position, never moving his eyes. Then, with an effort that signaled how his dog had gained middle age while Jock had been gone, he groaned and stood, then turned his back on Jock and sat down again. Sharon's gaze flickered between him and the dog, eyes wide. "Jerk," he muttered, then ignored the dog who was currently ignoring him, telling Sharon, "I wanted to let you know again how much I appreciate everything you and Gunny have done for me. I'll see you around, right?" He smiled at her, holding the expression until she gave him back one that trembled. "I'm going to be going through kiddy withdrawals, I know, so if you need a babysitter, you give me a call." She nodded and rose, coming to him and wrapping her arms around his chest. Tipping his head to the side, he bent and whispered, "Thank you. You guys saved me." She squeezed him and sucked in a stuttering breath.

Releasing her, he stepped back and waved to Cade. "Bu bye."

The smile on his face faded when she studied him seriously for a moment, then pulled her tiny features into a hard scowl before telling him, "'Lo." Raising a clenched fist, she flailed it in the air before opening it, raining pieces of cereal down on her head. "'Lo."

"Hello." He waved, then backed up another step. "Tank." The dog shifted but didn't turn. "Tank, come. Let's go, boy." Spine twisting, Tank looked over his shoulder, ass still firmly planted on the floor. "Dude, come on. You'll be back for a visit, promise." With a heavy sigh, Tank climbed to his feet and turned before padding over to Sharon. He butted her belly with his head, nearly taking her off her feet, then wound his way around her, slapping her legs with his tail on his way past. Nose to Kitten's toes, he snuffled until she giggled, then rested his chin on her tray for a moment, letting her beat her tiny fists against his head.

With another look at Jock, Tank shifted and stepped sideways until he was pressed up against the side of Cade's highchair. With a whine, he shoved his head underneath her tray, jostling the entire set-up until Sharon stepped over and pulled the release lever. Then he crowded closer, leaning sideways so he could get his head and neck in contact with Cade. The little girl scowled at Jock again, then bent over the dog, putting her mouth close to his ear, her fingers working through the folds of skin on his neck. "Bu bye."

Jesus. I've never seen a dog like this.

He'd contacted the breeder two weeks ago, trying to see if there'd be a puppy he could buy for Gunny. Maybe in six months or so, but nothing right now. Confronted by the connection Tank had with the kids, Jock wavered, his gut twisting while he tried to decide if this was the right thing. If it was just them, he wouldn't hesitate; Tank would have found a new forever home. But Tank eased something inside him, untangling the guilt he had for living when his entire patrol had died on the side of the road, thousands of miles from home. Without having Tank, he'd been a ghost, so far into the dark his fingers had grown to know the curve of his gun's trigger very well. Finding out the dog wasn't lost, was with good people, it had seemed too good to be true. Then finding out just how good Gunny was, and how he just got where Jock's head was, without judging, that had been an unspoken wish come true. Even with that, Tank had been the only thing that had gotten him through the past weeks. *I can't leave without him*.

"Come on, Tank. Time to go."

Another look over his shoulder at Sharon and Tank stepped back from Cade. The little girl seemed to suddenly understand what was happening, her face scrunching up, mouth going square as she cried, hiccupping through the words, "No. No go. Stay." Kitten picked up the cry, howling as if she were in pain. Cade held out a hand to Tank, her fingers tapping her palm in a broken wave. "'Lo. No bu bye. 'Lo."

"Sharon—" He started to say something, anything, but she waved her hand.

"Just go. I'll deal with this." Hand to the side of her belly, she walked to where Cade was still strapped into her chair.

"Tank, 'meer me!"

Sharon's voice was soft when she promised her daughter, "Oh, honey. It'll be okay."

No, it will never be okay.

***

Gunny

"Please, come home." Sharon's words were thick with pain, the sound of his girls crying echoing through the phone. "Honey, please."

"What's wrong?" He was already on the move, snapping his fingers at a prospect seated on a bucket by the office. Pointing back at his bay in the garage, he told the man, "Clean up for me. Everything in the box, lock it and then take the key to Red." Red was a member who managed the garage, and he'd make sure the expensive tools and parts were stowed correctly and safely. "Baby, what's wrong?" Sticking his head into the office, he told Red, "I gotta go." Getting a nod in response, he turned and let the door close behind him, heading out to his truck. "Baby, talk to me."

"It's just…we're all sad, Gunny. I can't stop crying and neither can the girls. We…I just need you."

"Fifteen minutes, I'll be there. Hold on, baby."

He could hear them when he parked the truck in the garage, picking out both girls' shrill voices, Sharon's a deeper rumble in contrast, but even through the monitor's speaker, he could tell she was barely holding everything together. *Fuck*. Inside, he followed the wails to the upstairs nursery, seeing Sharon seated on the ottoman between the cribs, face in her hands, shoulders shaking. Cade's eyes were swollen, and when she saw him, her unrelenting stream of "No bu bye," changed to "Da da, no go." Kitten's cries slowed, growing softer, but he could see from her red face that she'd been screaming for a while. Sharon lifted her head, and the pain in her face nearly took his legs from under him. *Girls will be okay, but she's too fragile for this bullshit right now*. He went straight to Sharon and picked her up, taking her place on the ottoman and settling her in his lap. Burying his face against the side of her head, he whispered, not sure if she could hear him over the kids, but hoping she'd be soothed in some way, "Baby. It'll be okay."

"What if it's not?" Her arms wound around his neck, holding tight as she pressed close to him. "Gunny, what if it's not?"

"It's not like Jock took the dog to the moon, honey." Cade stirred in her crib, rolling from her back to her belly, propping up on her elbows to stare at her parents. "He'll be back to visit. We got two dogs of our own, honey. Tank..." He paused, casting around for the right words. "...was just on loan for a good, long time."

"I know we have dogs." Sharon was still crying, cheek pressed to his chest. "But they aren't Tank." He glanced over and saw Cade's chin starting to quiver again. *Shit.* "Tank was...he was ours, Gunny. You said it, he was our dog. Why did you let Jock take him?"

Jesus. Sharon wasn't making any sense now, and he could feel her quivering, shaking like she had a fever. Worried, he lifted a hand to her cheek, finding it chilled instead of hot. "Baby." He stroked a hand down her back, pulling her closer. "Shhhhhhh. It's gonna be okay."

"What if it's not?" She returned to her previous question, and he felt her move, arching against his arm, pushing on his chest with both hands. Staring down into her face, the pain in her expression tore at him again, and he had to swallow hard to push the lump from his throat. "Gunny, I'm pregnant. What—" Fingers curled in his shirt, she pulled it away from his body and then thudded against his chest, impressing on him how deep her fear ran. "—if it's not?"

As he had been the night he brought Jock home from the hospital, Gunny was transported back to when Kitten was born, tasting the bright tears at the back of his throat at the sight of all the people waiting for him. Seeing Deke fearing to touch him, even knowing that all was well, too unsure what Gunny's reaction would be to the news to risk it. Deke's voice telling him, "They're both okay. Gonna be okay.

Sharon's good, and the baby's good, too. Bulldog's got her, and you know he does." Sharon's exhausted and exhilarated face, lying quietly in her hospital bed, staring in wonder at the newborn sleeping in the bassinette nearby.

"Bulldog." His voice was rough, scraping at his throat as he forced the words out. "Bulldog knows what happened. He's on guard with this little one. Bulldog—" He swallowed a shattered laugh at the idea that the man was called after a distant cousin of the mastiff. *About right*, he told himself. "—won't let anything happen to you, or to this baby, Sharon." He squeezed her with both arms, bending his neck to rest his forehead against hers. "He won't, and neither will I, baby. That's a promise you can count on."

She hiccupped, unblinking eyes staring into his. Gunny realized both girls had quietened. The room was silent except for the muffled jingling of dog tags as Rocky and Tank made their way upstairs. He watched her struggle with his words, trying to accept them but finding them wanting when held up against the depth of fear she had inside. A fear he hadn't known she carried, but it made sense. *She nearly died, our little girl with her.* After everything life had thrown at her, Sharon had proven herself strong time and time again, but he knew better than most how those experiences could mark a person.

Lips quivering, she flinched at the sound of her own voice when she asked, "You promise?"

He didn't pause, didn't have to think because if it could be pulled or pushed into life, he'd do it for her. "On my heart, I promise."

***

Walking out of the doctor's office, Gunny chuckled as he reached down to cup Sharon's elbow, steering her back onto the sidewalk. She had a roll of black and white pictures in her hands, holding them up in front of them. Gaze focused on the pixelated images, she lifted them and pointed with one trembling finger. "Look, honey. That's his winkie!"

"Fuck, Shar. Don't call it that."

Fingers working along the edges of the paper, she paused on another picture, her finger close to tracing along the curve of their little boy's face. "He's gonna be handsome, just like his daddy." Back to the other picture, she pointed again. "Winkie!"

Still chuckling when he folded himself behind the wheel of her van, he waited for her to reverently coil the images and tuck them into the depths of her purse before he asked, "You ready, baby?" She nodded, pulling her phone out and looking at the screen. "Everything okay?" She grinned, turning to show him the picture Jock had texted her, showing Tank, Tank, Rocky, Cade, and Kitten lying in a staggered row across the backyard. Jock had jumped at the chance to babysit, and when he walked in with Tank this morning, Gunny and Sharon ceased to exist for the two girls. "Looks like everyone's having a good time."

She looked at him, a soft expression on her face and he leaned close, brushing his mouth across hers. "We're havin' a boy."

"We are." She agreed on a whisper, her lips barely moving. "A little baby Lane. Injecting some testosterone into the Robinson household."

"Pretty sure the injecting part was done several months ago, babe." He chuckled at her scowl, seeing echoes of Cade's favorite expression. "God, you're so fuckin' beautiful. I love you, Sharon."

"Love you, too, big guy."

Bulldog had eased her fears, taking extra time during the ultrasound to show her the positioning of the placenta, optimal, according to him. He'd been practical, too, and Gunny knew Sharon appreciated it, talking through the statistics of a recurrence of the placenta breaking free like with Kitten. Those stats were low, so low it seemed an impossibility. But he'd addressed that, too, telling Sharon what to watch for and when to make a call. By the time they walked out of the office, she'd nearly been dancing circles around Gunny.

At home, Gunny found the removal of Tank the Larger from the household was only slightly less traumatic this time, Sharon being the only female not crying. He distracted the girls with the promise of a bath, and once they were clean, fed, and down for the night, he found Sharon curled into a corner of the couch, chin in the palm of one hand as she stared at the dark TV.

"Baby, whatcha watchin'?" He shoved his hands under her arms, lifting her as he sat and pulled her into his lap.

"Nothing." She yawned and leaned against him, nuzzling his chest. Chin to the top of her head, he held her and waited, knowing she wouldn't have stayed up for him if she didn't have something to say. "Gunny…" Her voice trailed off, then she continued. "How old are Tank and Rocky?"

He lifted a hand, smoothing his palm across his scalp. "Fuck, baby. I don't know. Less than ten. I got 'em the same year. Why?"

"I didn't get to grow up with a dog. I always wanted one." She wiggled and he groaned, enjoying the pressure of her ass rubbing on his cock as she snuggled into him. "What…how long do beagles and ratties live?"

Now he knew where she was going with this and he didn't like it. Didn't like the idea of losing his pups, but he also understood it was inevitable. Sharon was a planner, though, so it shouldn't be a surprise she was looking to the future. "Fifteen or so, depending on health. What are you dancing around, Shar?"

"Should we get a puppy now, before the baby comes?" She shrugged, the movement shifting her tits against his chest. "You know, before things get chaotic again?"

"You want a puppy? What kind?"

She was quiet for so long he wasn't sure what to expect. Then she showed him how much the big dog had impacted her, too. "Mastiff."

"I'll talk to PBJ tomorrow." She relaxed in his arms, revealing by that tiny motion how tense she'd been leading up to that request. "See what he can find for us. You sure you want to introduce a chewing, gnawing, barking puppy to the house?" Her head moved, hair dusting across his shoulders as she nodded. "Okay, baby. We'll see about a pup."

Chapter Five

Gunny walked into the garage and angled towards the office, planning on getting a cup of coffee before he started back to work on the custom rebuild he was doing for one of the Chicago members. As he moved through the building, he scanned the bays, noting they'd all been straightened and cleaned recently. He let his gaze travel beyond and his feet came to an abrupt stop. Jock was in the bay next to his, a bagger up on the lift. *What the hell?* The man seemed comfortable in the garage, looking over his shoulder as he chatted with one of the Rebel OGs, Tugboat, who was supervising a prospect's oil change. *Coffee first, then questions.*

Retrieving his tools, he glanced up from the workbench when Jock called his name. "Hey." Gunny picked up his coffee and opened another toolbox.

From the corner of his eye, he saw Jock rise to his feet from the low stool he had pulled up next to the lift.

"Is this okay?" Surprised by the question, Gunny turned to see Jock standing with shoulders slumped, fingers nervously turning a wrench this way and that. "Me being here, I mean."

"Yeah?" Shrugging, Gunny studied the man carefully. His face was drawn, features taut, and he didn't look rested. "How's it goin'? You doin' okay over at Domino's?" It had only been a couple of weeks since Jock had been over for dinner, and he hadn't looked like this then. "Brother, everything all right?"

Jock's lip curled, his body's instinctive attempt at control of his expression. Licking his lips, he nodded, turning half away. "Mighta missed a couple of appointments." Without looking around, Gunny quickly put up the few tools he'd laid out. Picking up his coffee, he waited, and Jock finally asked, "What?"

"Put your shit up. Let's go." Jock twisted to face Gunny, surprise on his face. "You know I'm not a patient man. I'm also not one to bullshit. You look like hell, brother. Tellin' me you missed an appointment would be bad, but you said a couple, which probably means four or five if I were to start digging. So, put up your shit, and let's go."

Jock swallowed hard but didn't move. Gunny saw Tugboat take a step closer to his back. "Gunny won't steer you wrong, Jock. He's throwin' you a lifeline, man. Don't turn your nose up at it." Jock's neck twisted and he turned to look at Tug, then back at Gunny, and he nodded. With jerky movements, he began gathering and dumping the tools into the boxes lining the bay. Gunny texted Sharon as he waited, smiling down at his phone when she responded in the affirmative immediately. Sipping his coffee, he noticed more than one member glancing their way, and even those small attentions seemed to ratchet up Jock's anxiety. He was thankful when it was all done, and without a word, he turned and led Jock outside, thumbing the button on his keychain to unlock his truck.

They'd been driving for a few minutes when Jock shifted in his seat, clearing his throat before asking, "How long does it take?"

"To get to the docs? Another ten minutes, brother. Sharon's called ahead. He's set, you're golden."

"No." Barked and loud, the edges of that single word were rough with anger, and Gunny glanced over to see Jock staring out the windshield. "I mean how long does it take before I stop fucking up everything? How long? How long before everything's back to normal, brother?"

Lie, and have Jock know he can't trust me to be straight with him? Or tell the truth, and wonder every day if it's the right decision? Gunny knew what he would have wanted, back when he was sitting where Jock was now, so he gave it to him straight, the unvarnished truth of how different their lives were from what came before.

"Never. Things will never be back to normal." Jock sucked in air, but Gunny pushed through, wanting to get all his words out before Jock interrupted him.

"What was normal before doesn't make sense now, not after what we've seen and done. After what we've survived. It's the surviving that does it, you know? Twists things so all the innocence is stripped away. It never goes back to what was normal. But if you work it, you can find a new normal that's just as good." He turned the wheel of the truck, steering the vehicle into the office parking lot. "Look at me. Ten years ago I was fucked up. So fucked up I was chasing ghosts through the forest. Strapped all the time, it's a fuckin' wonder I didn't shoot someone just for breathing some days. So fucked up, brother, if it weren't for people like Tug and Deke, like Mason and PBJ, I wouldn't be here talking in your ear. But now, I'm good. Got kid number three on the way, a boy, a namesake. Something to live for. Every breath is precious these days, and this, brother? This is my new normal. We just gotta help you find how to get to yours."

"It feels like I can't catch a break, brother. I get good, and then it all goes fuckin' sideways on me." Jock struggled with his seatbelt for a moment, the clasp defeating his fumbling fingers. "I just want...one fuckin' day where I feel like I did before."

"Ain't gonna get it." Gunny knew his words sounded bleak, because they were. But he had a longer view of things, a different perspective he could use to help shore up Jock's defenses. "What you will get is better every fuckin' day until you're no longer counting them. Better enough to know it was worth it. But whatever you're looking for in the past, you won't find it. Gotta move forward, soldier." He reached over and thumbed the button, releasing Jock's seatbelt. "Thing is, you aren't alone. I'm here. Tug's here. You got friends, brother."

"You think that can be enough?" Jock opened his door, slipping one foot out to rest on the ground. "Think I can get where you are?"

"I didn't do it alone. You gotta remember that, Jock. And yeah—" Gunny stood, closed his door and walked around the hood of the truck, meeting Jock by the bumper. "—I know you can get here, brother. I know you can."

The sky had darkened when they walked back to the truck, shading towards the deepest indigo along the horizon. Jock's movements were freer, his arms swinging naturally instead of stiff at his sides. Gunny felt good about the efforts of the day, and Sharon was insisting Jock join them for dinner. In the truck, Gunny waited a moment, flicking the radio seek button several times until he found a channel he liked. A commercial for dog food came on and prodded his memory, making him laugh.

"What?" Jock asked, resting one elbow on the windowsill.

"You. You're a miracle man, you know that?" Gunny pulled out of the lot, angling across the lanes to get to the turn that would take them home fastest. "Called PBJ a couple weeks ago, asked for the breeder's name where you got Tank. Called the breeder while I was waiting in the lobby just now. Wanna tell me what you think she had to say?"

Jock chuckled, the humor-filled sound relaxed. *Amazing what a single afternoon can do*, Gunny thought, then focused in on Jock's words. "If you were calling about pups, she probably told you she had a litter in the oven, due in about six weeks."

"Yeah, she said two pups were already spoken for. I'd led by sayin' I knew Tank's owner, and she gave me the joyous news that you were shoppin' for pups. Tell me, what in the hell are you gonna do with three mastiff dogs?" Gunny laughed, shaking his head.

"I'm not." Gunny glanced at him, seeing lines of tension back in his shoulders, lifting them by an inch. *Shit*. "Those pups are for you and Sharon. Cade and Kitten, mostly, but..." Jock took a deep breath. "Sharon needs a mastiff, man. These'll be full brother or sister to Tank, and the breeder is known for her dogs' dispositions. It won't make up for takin' your dog, but it's the best I can do."

"The fuck? You didn't take my dog. Tank's yours, man." The price the breeder quoted for a puppy was reasonable, given the quality, but the idea of Jock dropping that much money on a gift for him made Gunny uneasy. "Jesus. I called because Sharon wants a puppy. She was hoping to get one before the baby came, but the timing isn't going to work out right. Our boy is due just after Thanksgiving, and she said the pups won't be ready to go home until Christmas." He turned into his driveway, pulling up beside several bikes, recognizing three of them as belonging to Mason, Deke, and PBJ. "You can't...that's too much, man. I can buy my own dog."

Jock didn't move to exit the truck, and Gunny turned to meet his stare. They sat like that for a moment. Then Jock lifted his chin. "What price is my life? What price can you put on that, Gunny? We're friends. I feel that in my gut. You do shit like you did today for me without even thinking. Because that's who you are. That's what we are. I owe you more than I can even put words to, man. I owe you, not money, but my existence. You and Tank. I can't give him up, but I can gift you and your wife, your kids. I can gift you with something that might someday match in worth." Jock nodded towards the house, and Gunny turned to see the door open, Sharon standing in the light, rounded belly telling everyone how blessed he was. "She's amazing, and I hope to God I find one like her someday. Two pups? Doesn't put a dent in my debt—" Gunny opened his mouth to speak, but Jock shook his head. "I owe you. Pups will be a gift from me, to you and yours." The corner of Jock's lips quirked sideways, and he finished speaking as he got out of the truck, the slamming of his door putting a stop to any comebacks Gunny might have had. "I'm buyin' 'em. Done deal."

***

"Almost there, baby." Gunny reseated his grip on Sharon's leg, focusing in on her face as she breathed quickly, panting. "You're doing great."

The labor had progressed faster than he expected, but Bulldog didn't seem concerned, and Sharon was just glad things were more normal this time around. The contractions had woken her in the middle of the night, but there'd been plenty of time to call Mercy and Deke over to watch the girls. Once at the hospital, Gunny hadn't been surprised when the nurses started whispering about the bikers in the waiting room, because he knew Deke would have started calling as soon as Gunny and Sharon drove away.

"Okay, Sharon. Another big one coming up." Bulldog's voice came from near Gunny's hip, but he didn't turn to look. As long as he didn't see the man with his face all up in Sharon's pussy, he didn't have to kill him. "Monitor's showing this is a good one. I want a big, big push."

Sharon nodded, focused on Gunny's face as she echoed the doctor's countdown. "Three, two, one..." Her face twisted, fingers digging into his arm as she pulled herself upright. Gunny kept her leg up and steady, holding her open. The epidural meant she didn't have any pain, but it also meant she needed some assistance with the mechanical aspects of delivery.

"Doin' great, baby. So good. Such a good momma." She cut her eyes down to the doc, then back to him. "God, you're so fuckin' beautiful." He wiped the sweat from her forehead with the back of his hand, threading his fingers through her tangled hair. "My Rose of Sharon."

"Don't." She grunted the words, still pushing hard. "Say the eff-word."

Bulldog called a nurse over, telling Sharon, "Hold off a minute. Stop pushing, okay? He's crowning now."

"Baby, little Lane's preoccupied with getting his head smushed. He's not listening to me saying fuck."

"Don't call him that. His name's going to be Jason." This had been the ongoing disagreement in their house, starting as a joke, but then became something she had latched onto. Gunny smirked. *Not happenin', darlin'.*

"Okay, Sharon. Almost ready for another big push, okay?" The nurse stepped up on Sharon's other side, gaze flickering across the equipment with casual competence. "Doctor will tell you when."

"Baby, I ain't naming my only son after your brother." Gunny leaned in, pulling back when she snapped her teeth at him. "Shit, Sharon. What do we tell the girls? No biting."

"Jason." She took a deep breath. "Oh my God, I feel something. I think it's wearing off." Her panicked eyes glanced all around the room. "I feel something. Get him out. It's wearing off. I know it is."

"No, it's not, Sharon," Bulldog reassured her, as he had a dozen times in the last hour. "You're doing great."

"Lane, baby." He shifted until Sharon's knee was pressed to his side and rested his hand on her belly. "That's my boy in you. I want him to have my name."

"Okay, Momma. Give me another big push. Big, big push, okay?" Bulldog spoke as if they weren't having a serious conversation right over his head. Sharon locked gazes with Gunny again and mouthed the words as Bulldog counted down, "Three, two, one."

Eyes squeezed closed, she tucked her chin towards her chest, and strained, face red. Sweat trickled down her temples and Gunny stroked the side of her face, other hand on her belly, feeling the muscles contracting strongly. He felt a shift when the baby moved, Sharon's stomach jerking slightly as Bulldog told her, "His head's out. Give me a minute to adjust for his shoulders. Gunny, brother, you got a linebacker here."

Dragging in huge breaths, Sharon's head sagged backwards against the pillow. Eyes closed, she whispered something Gunny didn't catch, so he leaned forwards. "What, baby?"

"Joshua." Gunny froze, trying not to smile at what Sharon was saying. "Joshua Wade. Yours and Ace's middle names." She lifted her head and glared at him. "I. Feel. Something."

"Okay, Sharon. Finish line's in sight. Another push, not as big." The nurse had returned to stand beside Bulldog, a towel in her gloved hands.

"I feel something, too." Gunny stared at her. "Love you, my Rose of Sharon." She held his gaze this time through the push, and they were still staring into each other's eyes when the sound of a baby's first hiccupping cries filled the room.

***

"Gunny, can you get the door?" Sharon's voice filtered through the Christmas music she had playing. She was upstairs, and he knew that, which meant when the doorbell rang and the dogs barked, he was already on his way towards the door.

Rolling his eyes, he responded, "Sure thing, baby. Soon as I finish this movie." He was grinning up when her head popped into view, eyebrows drawn nearly to her hairline snapping down into a fierce frown as she took in his expression. She mouthed the word, "Asshole," to him and he laughed. "Sharon, don't call your babies' daddy an asshole."

"Honey, don't say the A-word in front of the kids." Swinging her hand out, she indicated Cade and Kitten playing on the floor, and Josh in his portable crib set-up nearby. Shaking her head, she disappeared to finish getting ready. They were hosting a bunch of the Fort

Wayne Rebels for a party tonight, all the couples with kids would be arriving early and then heading home in time for Santa to come visiting at their houses.

"You started it," he called up the stairs as he opened the door. "Hey, brother," he greeted PBJ who had his arms folded awkwardly around a box. Something solid hit Gunny's thighs and he looked down to see Tank actively wiping slobber on his jeans. "Hey, big guy." He leaned down in time to catch a swipe of Tank's massive tongue across his face, standing up laughing as he wiped with one hand. "Jesus, asshole."

"The A-word," Sharon said from behind him, and he looked to see both PBJ and Jock grinning. "Don't say it." She leaned around Gunny and ruffled Tank's ears, capturing the dog's face in both hands and bending to press a kiss to the top of his head. "Who's a good dog?"

"Y'all come in," Gunny said, shuffling Sharon and the dog to one side. A moment later, Tank abandoned her as Cade caught sight of him, her excited cries of "Tank, Tank," taking precedence. "Whatcha got there, PBJ?"

"Just carryin' 'em for Jock." PBJ turned, shoving the box into Jock's arms. "Cade, what about your Unka Pee? Got a little love left for me?" Jock stepped inside, and Gunny closed the door, reaching out to pull Sharon close to his side. He expected waterworks from her, not just because she was only three weeks past giving birth to their son, but because of what Jock had in the box. They'd worked this out between them, keeping it a secret from Sharon after Gunny had let her down easy that the breeder wouldn't have puppies until after Josh was born. "Kitten," PBJ called, laughter rising from both girls at whatever he was doing, "Gimme some belly." Giggles competed with the sound of wet raspberries in the background as Jock stared down at Sharon.

Gunny glanced behind him and froze. Tank was actively shoving a kitchen chair across the floor, angling it towards Josh's crib. There was no way the little fold up piece of furniture would support the dog's weight, but just as he was about to open his mouth to scold the dog, Tank got the chair in place and put his front feet on the seat, leaning on the side of the crib to get his head down to where Josh lay sleeping. Even from here Gunny could see the dog's ribs rise and fall with a sigh. Another moment and Tank lifted his head and looked across the room, clambering down from the chair to fall with a groan beside Cade.

"What's in the box? You didn't get the girls a gift, did you? Having you here is all the gift they need. Cade misses you so." Sharon looped one arm around Gunny's waist, slipping a finger into one of his belt loops. "I'm so glad you could come tonight."

"I got...it's for the girls, and Josh. But..." Jock's voice trailed off and he shifted the box, a sliding sound coming from inside followed by the softest whimper. "It's mostly for you, Sharon."

Her head tipped to the side, pressing into Gunny's ribs. "Me?"

Gunny glanced across the room again. PBJ was having a semiserious conversation with Kitten, passing a toy back and forth between them. She was their giving child, always handing over whatever she had in an effort to make someone smile. Like her mother, she found strays of all kinds and took them in, whether it was a broken toy or a lost kid in the mall. Her goal in life seemed to be to make things better. Cade was their thinker. She would study things and people in a way that made you believe even though she was not quite three, she was marking what was said and done. She loved puzzles, too. Sharon said she was a lot like her daddy, and Gunny grinned. Right now, she was sprawled out across Tank's back, mouth to his ear, whispering her thousand secrets of the day.

Jock hefted the box again. "Can I sit this down? It'll be easier to show you." Sharon nodded and stepped back, Gunny moving with her to give Jock ample room. Jock stared down at the box as he set it on the floor, eyes fixed on the flaps held in place by his fingers. "When I got the letter from my wi—my ex-wife, I was pissed, so pissed. We went out on patrol that night, and all I could think of was a hundred versions of 'how dare she.' She'd taken something I wanted more than life, and torn it away." His gaze flickered up then down, too fast to have registered anything other than Sharon's sadness. "I knew she was carrying a boy. My son. We had picked out names and everything, video chatted during the ultrasound so I could see him. I couldn't be there, but she was strong, and it was all going to be okay. That's what I'd held tight to. Then she tore it all away. 'Not your child' and 'sorry' in her letter kept running through my head. We're on patrol, and all I can think of is her and how to fix it. How to fix it and get her back, get my family back."

He looked at Gunny, who had heard most of this story before. Most, but not all, not the important parts. "You know how it is. You need to be focused. Gotta be on point, all the time. I wasn't on point. My entire world had slid sideways, and I wasn't on point. Then the world blew up around me, and people died." Tears welled in Jock's unblinking eyes; this was a confession he felt he had to make. "It's taken me a long, long time to figure out they didn't die because of me. I wasn't in the lead, wasn't even on the side the attack came from. But I believed if I'd just been paying attention, I could have saved everyone." He swallowed hard as Gunny reached out and rested a hand on his shoulder, gripping tightly. "It wasn't my fault." Intended as a statement, still his voice rose on the last word, compelling Gunny to answer him.

"No, brother. It wasn't your fault."

A scratching sound came from the box, and Jock looked down, swiping a forearm across his face. "I got back and found out Tank was gone, too. But, he wasn't. He was here, waiting on me." Jock breathed deeply, shoulders rising and falling with the motion. "He was here, and he was paying attention. Your world started sliding sideways, but he caught you."

Sharon answered this time, and that was right, because it had happened to her. "Yeah, he did. He's a good dog."

"He *is* a good dog." Jock opened the top of the box to reveal two dark lumps nestled into the blanket covering the bottom. "A really good dog. These are his brothers." Looking up at Sharon, Jock told her, "I got them for you. They're not replacements for Tank, but...I think you need them."

***

Jock

He leaned his shoulders against the wall, watching with a smile as Gunny's terrier rolled to his back, growling playfully at the puppy who was trying to scale his side. The mastiff pup weighed nearly as much as Rocky did, but that wasn't dissuading the terrier from establishing who was the dominant one. For now, at least.

Sharon was perched on Gunny's lap, talking animatedly as she leaned far over so she could pick up her water from beside the chair they were in. Gunny's big hand held her secure, wrapping around the side of her waist. No way would he let her fall, and she knew it, trusting him to keep her safe. The woman she was talking to, Bex, was married to one of the Rebels. He and Brute had chased up some acquaintances in common, running through deployments and barracks-mates, laughing at how some things never changed.

He sighed. This was a good life, one he could get used to. Mason looked up from across the room, his sleeping daughter in his arms. Their gazes caught and Mason lifted his chin while Jock nodded. They'd had a fruitful conversation earlier about Jock wanting to join the Rebels. This whole group felt right; it was more a family than anything else, at least from what he could see. From some of the stories told at the bar when the women weren't near, he knew it was more, too. But this was what he needed most of all.

Light laughter came tripping from the kitchen, and he turned to watch several of the women making their way back into the living room carrying drinks in their hands. One by one they broke away from the gaggle, going to sit next to kids or men. One woman continued on, aiming directly to where he stood. Jock looked to his left and right, trying to decide where she belonged, but he'd picked this spot to stand because it was slightly isolated.

"Hey," she said, turning to lean against the wall next to him. She held out a beer by the neck, an unmistakable offer. "I'm Silly."

"You are?" He reached out and took it, trying to remember how to flirt, because she'd made the first move and clearly telegraphed her interest. "How silly are you?"

Dark eyes dancing, she smiled up at him, pushing her light purple hair away from her face. Flicking a fingertip directly between her breasts, pulling his attention to her chest, she laughed as she said, "No, silly. I'm Silly." Tipping her head to the side, she pulled that fingertip up to her throat, to her chin, and then positioned it on her nose. His eyes followed the movement, and he focused on her face when she clarified things. "As in, that's my name."

"Oh." *Stupidest response in my life.* "I like silly things." *Only slightly better, Jesus.* "I'm Jock."

***

Gunny

Gunny looked down when Sharon's elbow gouged him painfully in the ribs. "Ow. Fuck, honey."

"Don't say the eff-word in front of our guests." By now her scolding was routine and he grinned at her. "Lookie, Jock's making a new friend."

He scanned the room, finding Jock against the far wall, beer in hand. A slow grin spread across his face when he saw who stood next to the man. Sylvia, or Silly, as she preferred to be called, was a tattoo artist from Chicago, down for Christmas to visit her niece, Carmela. Carmela had hooked up with Hurley, and the couple were spending the next six months here, after being in Mexico for the last several. "You don't say?"

Sharon gripped his chin in her hand, angling his face down. "Did you set that up?'

"Who me?" Dipping his neck, he brushed his mouth across hers. "You like the pups?"

She dropped her forehead to his chest with a thud. "God, Gunny. I can't imagine how much they cost him." Lifting her head, she made a face, eyes wide. "Thousands." He nodded. "You already tried to pay him back, didn't you?" He nodded again, and she rolled her eyes. "Yes, they're adorable and I love them. The girls...did you see Cade's face when she saw them? God, I love her."

Gunny kissed her again and cradled her head to his shoulder, letting her hide her tears for a moment. He swept the room with his gaze, taking in the family he'd built. Near the Christmas tree, Tank lay on the edge of a blanket spread as a pallet, a dozen or more kids in tangled piles around him. He was looking at Gunny, his tail beating a steady thump against the floor. Gunny grinned when Rocky dashed up to Tank the Larger, paused a moment to look over his shoulder, and then neatly hopped over the big dog, leaving the chasing pups stymied by the mountain of fur and bone in their path. A moment later they were gnawing on Tank's jowls, tripping over his paws as they tugged and growled.

"Hey, Sharon?" At his soft call, she lifted her head and looked at him. "I want two more."

Eyes wide, she stared. "Puppies? We've already got four dogs, Gunny. Two more? That's too much."

"Kids."

Time seemed to stop and he waited for her response. She swallowed and opened her mouth, then swallowed again. "Kids?"

He nodded.

"Two?"

He nodded.

"*Fuck me.*"

"Baby," he scolded through his grin. "Don't say the eff-word." Dipping close, he put his lips to her ear and whispered, "Josh is three weeks old, means you got three weeks to rest up, baby. Then," he kissed the side of her head, "it's on."

~ Fini ~

THANK YOU FOR READING *Gunny's Pups!*

I hope you enjoyed this story featuring Gunny, a returning character in the Rebel Wayfarers MC world.

ABOUT THE AUTHOR

Raised in the south, MariaLisa learned about the magic of books at an early age. Every summer, she would spend hours in the local library, devouring books of every genre. Self-described as a book-a-holic, she says "I've always loved to read, but then I discovered writing, and found I adored that, too. For reading...if nothing else is available, I've been known to read the back of the cereal box."

Also by MariaLisa deMora

Alace Sweets

A dark thriller, this book is not a light read. Filled with edge-of-your-seat suspense, this intense story commands the reader's attention as it drives towards the explosive ending. Alace Sweets is a vigilante serial killer, with everything that implies and is sure to trip all your triggers. Be ready.

At seventeen, Alace Sweets turned a corner in her life, taking the wrong shortcut home from school.

Resisting the harsh knowledge her attackers will never be made to pay for their actions, Alace takes a stand. Justice must be served, and if fate's scales are out of balance, she's determined to set things right as best she can.

When the laws of men fail, the rules of Alace prevail.

5-Star Reviews for Alace Sweets

"deMora has a superb story-line and exceptional character development. All of her characters have such depth that will intrigue the reader..."
~Turning Another Page

"Hot, sweet, dark thriller."
~Beth D

"It will keep you on the edge of your seat and give you chills."

~Escape Reality Book Blog

"Disturbing, haunting, sickly; yet hot, sexy and heart racing!"
~Amanda L

"From the first page [deMora] pulls you into the world she has created and you do not even try to escape..."
~Little Shop of Readers Blog

"A must read for all those dark, gritty romance fans out there."
~Sweet & Spicy Reads

"You will find yourself so drawn into the story that the outside world is blocked out and your locking the doors and turning on all the lights."
~Danena F

"Don't judge me for bonding with a vigilante serial killer, she's more than what she does."
~iScream Books

"Thrilling...chilling...full of suspense, nail biting edge of your seat excitement."
~Tracey H

"Every time MariaLisa deMora picks up her pen (or opens her computer), she creates characters you want to believe in."
~Gail S

"Intriguing dark storyline, beautiful love story and nail-biting conclusion, what more could a reader ask for?"
~Manda M

"This book takes you a dark and twisted ride that is gripping..."
~Renee Entress' Blog

"This book is dark and gritty and I literally had to take a day off from reading it because it's that intense."
~My Girlfriend's Couch

"This is my favourite book so far from this author ... I recommend this book if you enjoy dark romantic thrillers."
~Cheekypee Reads and Reviews

"There's not enough stars to give this book and 5 just doesn't really do it justice!"
~DeLane C

"I couldn't put this book down from page one! Tried to stop & go to bed but couldn't sleep thinking about Alace and got up & finished the book."
~Debbie M

"MariaLisa DeMora, wordsmith that she is, made this a story of the enlightenment of a woman and finding love in a life where she has had none."
~Kat W

"Whatever deep dark trench [deMora] pulled a character like Alace from should be revisited again and often."
~Confessions of a Serial Reader

ADDITIONAL SERIES AND BOOKS

Please note that books in a series frequently feature characters from additional books within that series. If series books are read out of order, readers will twig to spoilers for the other books, so going back to read the skipped titles won't have the same angsty reveals.

Rebel Wayfarers MC series:

Mica, #1
A Sweet & Merry Christmas, short story #1.5
Slate, #2
Bear, #3
Jase, #4
Gunny, #5
Mason, #6
Hoss, #7
Harddrive Holidays, short story #7.5
Duck, #8
Biker Chick Campout, short story #8.5
Watcher, #9
A Kiss to Keep You, novella #9.25
Gun Totin' Annie, short story #9.5
Secret Santa, short story #9.75
Bones, #10
Gunny's Pups, novella #10.25
Never Settle, short story #10.5
Not Even A Mouse, short story #10.75

Fury, #11
Christmas Doings, #11.25
Gypsy's Lady, #11.5
Cassie, #12
Road Runner's Ride, novella #12.5

Occupy Yourself band series:

Born Into Trouble, #1
Grace In Motion, #2 (TBD)
What They Say, #3 (TBD)

Neither This, Nor That series:

This Is the Route Of Twisted Pain, #1
Treading the Traitor's Path: Out Bad, #2
Trapped by Fate on Reckless Roads, #3 (TBD)

Other Books:

With My Whole Heart
Alace Sweets
Hard Focus

More information available at mldemora.com.